ꗃ The Best Revenge

HARDSCRABBLE BOOKS — FICTION OF NEW ENGLAND

Laurie Alberts, *Lost Daughters*

Laurie Alberts, *The Price of Land in Shelby*

Thomas Bailey Aldrich, *The Story of a Bad Boy*

Robert J. Begiebing, *The Adventures of Allegra Fullerton; Or, A Memoir of Startling and Amusing Episodes from Itinerant Life*

Robert J. Begiebing, *Rebecca Wentworth's Distraction*

Anne Bernays, *Professor Romeo*

Chris Bohjalian, *Water Witches*

Dona Brown, ed., *A Tourist's New England: Travel Fiction, 1820–1920*

Joseph Bruchac, *The Waters Between: A Novel of the Dawn Land*

Joseph A. Citro, *DEUS-X*

Joseph A. Citro, *The Gore*

Joseph A. Citro, *Guardian Angels*

Joseph A. Citro, *Lake Monsters*

Joseph A. Citro, *Shadow Child*

Sean Connolly, *A Great Place to Die*

John R. Corrigan, *Center Cut*

John R. Corrigan, *Snap Hook*

Pamala-Suzette Deane, *My Story Being This: Details of the Life of Mary Williams Magahee, Lady of Colour*

J. E. Fender, *The Private Revolution of Geoffrey Frost*

J. E. Fender, Audacity, *Privateer Out of Portsmouth*

J. E. Fender, *Our Lives, Our Fortunes*

Dorothy Canfield Fisher (Mark J. Madigan, ed.), *Seasoned Timber*

Dorothy Canfield Fisher, *Understood Betsy*

Joseph Freda, *Suburban Guerrillas*

Castle Freeman, Jr., *Judgment Hill*

Frank X. Gaspar, *Leaving Pico*

Robert Harnum, *Exile in the Kingdom*

Ernest Hebert, *The Dogs of March*

Ernest Hebert, *Live Free or Die*

Ernest Hebert, *The Old American*

Sarah Orne Jewett (Sarah Way Sherman, ed.),
The Country of the Pointed Firs and Other Stories

Raymond Kennedy, *Ride a Cockhorse*

Raymond Kennedy, *The Romance of Eleanor Gray*

Lisa MacFarlane, ed., *This World Is Not Conclusion:
Faith in Nineteenth-Century New England Fiction*

G. F. Michelsen, *Hard Bottom*

Don Mitchell, *The Nature Notebooks*

Anne Whitney Pierce, *Rain Line*

Kit Reed, *J. Eden*

Rowland E. Robinson (David Budbill, ed.),
Danvis Tales: Selected Stories

Roxana Robinson, *Summer Light*

Rebecca Rule, *The Best Revenge: Short Stories*

Catharine Maria Sedgwick, *The Linwoods;
or "Sixty Years Since" in America*

R. D. Skillings, *How Many Die*

R. D. Skillings, *Where the Time Goes*

Lynn Stegner, *Pipers at the Gates of Dawn: A Triptych*

Theodore Weesner, *Novemberfest*

W. D. Wetherell, *The Wisest Man in America*

Edith Wharton (Barbara A. White, ed.),
Wharton's New England: Seven Stories and Ethan Frome

Thomas Williams, *The Hair of Harold Roux*

Suzi Wizowaty, *The Round Barn*

The Best Revenge

S H O R T   S T O R I E S

Rebecca Rule

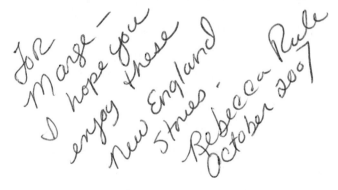

For Marge —
I hope you
enjoy these
New England
Stories.
Rebecca Rule
October 2007

University of New Hampshire Press
Durham, New Hampshire

Published by University Press of New England
Hanover and London

For my friends — with edges like

sedges — especially Sarah and Peg,

who inspire with the strength they

found when they needed it.

University of New Hampshire Press
Published by University Press of New England
One Court Street, Lebanon, NH 03766
www.upne.com

© 1995 by Rebecca Rule

First University of New Hampshire Press/UPNE paperback edition 2004

Printed in the United States of America   5   4   3   2   1

CIP data appear at the end of the book

C O N T E N T S

Yankee Curse   1

The Best Revenge   9

Lindy Lowe at Bat   22

Minna Runs for Selectman   34

The Widow and the Trapper   49

Jim's Boat   61

Fishing with George   71

Three   80

Marymay's Eyes   93

Peach Baby Food Sandwiches   104

Parasites   115

Etta Walks   126

Walking the Trapline   133

Saturday Night at the Hi-View Drive-In   143

Eva on the Beach   156

Bonfire   161

The White Room   168

The Fisher Cat   174

Ada Among the Dogs   185

Acknowledgments   195

About the Author   197

⚑ The Best Revenge

✠ Yankee Curse

At School District Meeting, Miranda knits.

May your neighbors steal from your wood pile, Mort Wallace.

The points of her flexi-needle slide in and out of the heavy burgundy wool.

May they incinerate their garbage in a barrel at your property line. And may the wind blow in your direction.

She counts seventeen stitches. She re-counts, eighteen stitches. She remembers the musk of burning garbage, the red smoke blowing over, ash falling like snow.

May you choke on the smoke.

She maintains tension with her right index finger. That's the trick of it, isn't it, the pressure against callused flesh of wool flowing over.

May the ashes fall hot on your bald head.

Miranda's thick hair—bands of gray and white—beehives in mysterious swirls that amaze the young parents sitting one row behind her. When she lifts her chin, the back of her neck straightens, and the lines of her jaw smooth into youth.

She knits. Yarn loops her forefinger like a bloody slice.

Mort Wallace stands, but not to speak. He sidles to the PTA concession for a refill from the coffee urn—his fifth since the meeting started. The PTA volunteers are beginning to look at him strangely. He throws coins on the counter, then opens his lips to suction in the hot liquid—black and rainbow skimmed.

At the front of the gym Kaye Elbow, school board chair,

speaks. The microphone amplifies the quaver in her voice. Mort Wallace will destroy this young woman if he can: Miranda has seen that in his cold, deep-set eyes—eyes that, over the years, seem to have sunk deeper and deeper into his skull. His hand tests the strength of the Styrofoam cup. His nostrils take in the steam.

Miranda knits faster, drops one stitch, corrects, knits on, drops another. She has hated Mort Wallace since childhood. Her parents hated his parents, so she in turn hated him. That is the way of it in these small towns—to hate by tradition. But make no mistake, Mort Wallace has earned his share. Even Miranda's Aunt Lou (who had a kind word for everyone) said of having been Mort's Red Cross swimming instructor when he was a boy: "I should have drowned him when I had the chance."

She was referring to Mort's meanness. He is an opinionated man. Everyone in town has opinions, most of them set in granite. Mort's opinions, though, are veined with meanness. He stands *against* on every issue; *against*, vehemently and with nothing but contempt and harsh words for those who stand *for*. He is a mean man. See it in his face. Hear it in his voice. Know it in the way his children leave home as soon as they graduate high school and never come back.

May your children spite you with their choices. May they abandon you in old age.

Know it in the way his first wife disappeared without warning—leaving her own babies, as though she saw in them what she loathed in her husband.

Know it in the way his followers—he has a few—peck at the grains of his meanness like chickens following the feeding pail.

May your chickens lay thin-shelled eggs, Mort Wallace. May skunks nest under the hen house. May raccoons scream at midnight in the pine tree that scratches your bedroom window.

Miranda does not invoke rabies—nor does she ever wish, even in the secret pocket of her heart, for the death of her enemy. "Curse them in this life," said her Gramma Annie, from whom she learned the art of the well-directed curse. Gramma Annie, whom Miranda much admired, said death was an evil call and unworthy.

Though they've never spoken, Miranda has admired Kaye Elbow from the first time she saw her smiling down a heckler, too naive, it seemed, even to realize she was being heckled. Miranda admires Kaye Elbow's broad dark face and the way emotions skitter across it like bird shadows on the water. Miranda, who has no children, has long been ripe with maternal instincts, which come on strong for Kaye Elbow (her heart quickens, her mouth tastes metal) when Mort Wallace's hand shoots up, raised stiff-armed from the shoulder, like a schoolboy in need of a bathroom pass. His shoulders round forward. His chest—under thin, checked flannel—appears to fold in on itself, yet there is enough air in those folded lungs to give his voice a boom that turns all heads: "Yes, I *do* have a question for you, Madam Chairman."

Miranda's husband Everett, God rest his soul, said this about Mort Wallace: "He's got two gears—neutral and steaming mad." When Mort speaks in public, it is always in anger. Some in the crowd lower their heads, embarrassed, hoping the storm will blow through quickly. Some exchange gleeful looks: *Mort's gonna give it to 'em now!* Some want to fight back. Some want to shoot him down and watch him, winged, spiral splat into the water.

Miranda expects Mort acts even worse at home. She pities his second wife—the nonentity, step-mother to his grown and gone children. They say she is an active alcoholic who never leaves the house after 6 P.M. Of course, Mort is out practically every evening; stirring up trouble at selectmen's meetings, bud-

get committee, planning board, Save-Our-Wetlands. (He op-
poses wetlands.) Wherever there is trouble to be stirred, he
stirs it.

In summer, Mort Wallace's second wife tends a garden of
annuals along the walkway in front of the house: ageratum,
marigold, cleome, and masses of white petunias. Walking by,
Miranda sometimes sees her kneeling on the bricks, dragging
at the weeds with eager hands.

"Hello," Miranda says if their eyes meet. "Hello," Mort Wallace's second wife says back.

Miranda knits to the rhythm of her curse.

*May your second wife find a sharp tongue in the bottle she
loves and slice you with it.*

Miranda knits the left sleeve of a burgundy cardigan for the
man in the old-folks-home who is still her father though he no
longer knows her. This is a curse she would never levy, not
even on Mort Wallace: to live too long. The rhythm of her
stitches falters when she thinks of her good-hearted father,
beyond suffering they say, but *they* don't know, do they?
The rhythm of her stitches falters when she thinks of her
own strong, kind Everett struck down by a weak heart before
his time, and Mort Wallace, who never did a bit of good for
anybody in this town, living on and on like some tough old
bramble dug in so deep you can't kill it no matter how many
times you mow it down.

"Mort Wallace was a bully as a child and he's still a bully,"
Aunt Lou said.

"Just like his old man," her father said.

"He's a phenomenon," Everett said.

Mort Wallace didn't much bother Everett, not even during
Everett's four terms on the Board of Selectmen. Though once,
when Mort accused him outright and in public of fraud, Everett did get riled. "You do get some funny ideas, Mr. Wallace,"

Everett said, out of his chair and advancing. "I'm not much of a one for lawyers and lawsuits, but you say that again, and I'm on the phone, misterman." Everett's thick finger pushed into Mort's concave chest, "And I'm going to find me a lawyer."

It hurt her to see Everett attacked. She curls her knitting in her lap and lowers her head. So far the discussion at this School District Meeting has been civil, back-and-forth talk among good people trying hard to come to terms, trying to find a balance. Mort Wallace will try to change all that with his old trick of setting neighbor against neighbor.

May your neighbors' children BB your windows, cherry-bomb your mailbox, siphon your gas and deflate your tires. May the little ones pierce your rest with their shrieks.

She studies the rich color of the sweater that will eventually be her father's but remains hers until the last tail is tied off.

May your dog bark on and on. May she someday turn on you without warning. May she haunt your dreams when she's gone.

Miranda studies the fine, even stitches, row upon row, interlocking like the fingers of clasped hands.

May the words you are about to fire at Kaye Elbow turn like a boomerang stick and strike you between your cold, depthless eyes.

Mort's voice carries, loud and sharp as gunfire.

May your shingles curl and your clapboards peel.

Miranda lets the hum in her head turn Mort Wallace's words to gibberish. *May your sills rot under your feet.* She fingers her knitting, hefts accomplishment. She holds the sleeve out for scrutiny, a sharp eye for flaw. But she sees no flaw. She sees a perfect burgundy plain. *May carpenter ants turn your beams to powder.* A stranger in the next chair pokes her and whispers, "That's coming along good?" Miranda meets the stranger's eyes, and he is struck by how beautiful her eyes are, like clear water flowing over a mica-flecked ledge.

Kaye Elbow smiles at Mort Wallace, a tense dark figure lean-ing hard into the cement-block wall. His arms are crossed so tight it looks painful. Kaye is new to the board, chair by default (no one else would take the job), and has been warned about this man and how he would try to influence the vote with a hard, fast twist of reality. "What gives you people the gall," Mort Wallace says, "to ask us hard-working taxpayers to cough up more money. You didn't manage your budget—plain and simple. Maybe you didn't know how. Maybe you didn't want to. Maybe you didn't care. Maybe you're stupid. I won't say you're a bunch of crooks—I'd like to but I won't."

"I'm sorry, sir," Kaye Elbow says. "Would you state your name for the record?"

"You don't know who I am? Tell her who I am, Robert," he says to one of the other school board members.

"You tell her," Robert says.

May a rat die between the studs of your bedroom wall.

Everett always said, "Mort Wallace has his followers, but they're none too many and none too bright." When Everett chaired the Board of Selectmen, he knew how to handle Mort's kind: "Sit down," he'd say, "we've heard enough," with a rap of the gavel. And if they didn't sit down, he'd suggest, mildly, "You want to step outside then, and settle it in town hall yard?" No one ever took him up on the offer, especially not Mort.

"For the record, my name is Morton Wallace. Is that clear enough for you, honey?"

Kaye Elbow says in a high, steady voice (she is no longer smiling): "Quite clear, honey. Now let me clarify something." She holds one white index card in her hand. She reads from it. The School District, she explains, is not in deficit and can-not, by law, enter into deficit. The board is simply presenting the facts so voters can decide how to proceed, considering the special-education overrun, the hike in insurance, and the fact that the furnace is so far gone it can't be fixed and winter coming on.

She looks straight at Mort Wallace, tilts her head sweetly: "And by the way, I don't feel that any particular gall is required to stand before you. I'm just doing the job I was elected to do."

Mort Wallace's eyes darken. They are as dark as scorched pine. His face is gray, the hard lines deepened by his freshly inflamed anger and the artificial light.

Miranda watches the pulse in the cording of his throat. She sees how the cuff of his shirt hangs at his wrist, how his belt is freshly notched. He has smoked too many cigarettes and slipped too many shots of whiskey into his bottomless cup of coffee. More importantly, a terrible backwash of his own venom has poisoned him, is punishing him more than her mild curses ever could.

Now, she raises her hand, full of knitting. An umbilical cord of burgundy yarn trails into the tapestry bag at her feet. The sleeve is a burgundy flag. Recognized by the chair, Miranda stands: "Mrs. Coffey—Miranda Coffey—some of you know me." She reminds herself to speak right up. "I realize you folks are doing the best you can. You're working awful hard and you've got figures to back up what you're saying. So I'm going to vote the money you asked for."

From the corner of her eye, she sees Mort with his hand in the air again. She turns to face him. She addresses her kind lie directly to him: "Mort Wallace, I know you mean well," she says. She holds her knitting tight to her chest, and takes a long breath. "But there's no need for you to be talking that way to these good people. Sit down, now; we've heard enough."

Since he has no chair, Mort can't sit down. But Miranda

sees that he would if he could. She sees it in the way his mouth opens and closes, in the way he flattens into the cement-block wall and fades like old paint. Everett would approve.

Miranda sits down. The stranger next to her touches her elbow. The young mother behind her leans forward and whispers: "I'm glad you spoke up."

Miranda knits.

⚏ The Best Revenge

At pottery class Catherine sculpts the head of her enemy. She works at a small table in a shadowy corner behind the wood stove, separate from the other potters. Lief, their teacher, has stoked the stove, though it is still August, a cool August night after a day of rain. The barn is damp and cold. Catherine studies the red glow where the rusty stove pipe mates with the cast iron. She studies the curve of Lief's wide back as he bends to slide pine kindling into the flames through the open door, a quick, hot fire, his face red in its glow.

The clay smoothes under her fingers.

The assignment was to create a pinch pot—a dollop of clay flattened by hand, then pinched at the edges into a shallow bowl. But she isn't making a pinch pot. Lately, she hasn't been very good at following instructions. The half-pound of clay wants to be a head, not a pot. It wants to be the head of Lucy Dahl.

Catherine recalls their first meeting, when Lucy crossed the property line, from her yard to theirs. Her nylon top was too pink; her beige chinos too tight. Her hair, also beige, was combed into points at the ears. Matthew made one more cut — then set the saw down, still whirring. He was building a rail for the front steps. ("I hope you're not putting that up for me," Catherine had told him, "because I don't need it.")

Matthew smiled at Lucy Dahl. Who could resist that easy

smile—the flash of white, the protruding eyetooth bending his lip? Who could resist that snaggle-toothed smile?

Lucy could.

Catherine, behind him, touched his neck with a cold beer. He reached back for her hand, for the beer, still smiling, puzzled.

Lucy didn't want a beer. She had a message to deliver and she delivered it. "Traditionally," she said, "we each keep to our own stretch of waterfront."

Matthew sprawled on the steps. He slid the moist can between his bare knees. "Huh?"

"People swim in front of their own house instead of the neighbor's," she said. "That way there's no trouble. It's common courtesy."

She mentioned no specific transgressions, but Catherine knew exactly what she meant. The day before, Randy and his inflatable dragon, Puff, had drifted in front of the Dahl house, contaminating, no doubt, Lucy's personal acre of lake water.

"Not too deep," Catherine had called to her son from the lawn chaise—her book open on her lap. She doesn't read when he's in the water. She thinks about reading, picks out a sentence or two, but mainly she watches her boy. "Come in a little. What did I just tell you?" Puff's fluorescent wings hugged Randy's waist.

Lucy had appeared a few minutes earlier on her front porch, a silhouette behind the screen. Though Lucy obviously saw them—Catherine in the chaise with her Panama hat and baggy shorts, Randy at play in the water—she pretended not to. Maybe she thought they hadn't spotted her. Maybe, like a heron in water weeds, she believed herself perfectly camouflaged. Her only movement was, from time to time, to raise a tall glass slowly to her lips.

Randy paddled up and down the shore in about two feet of

water. He practiced his kicks, searched for frogs in the weeds, scared them away with his splashing and shrieking: "Mom—I saw a fish!" "Mom, watch what I can do!" "Mom, swim with me!"

But Catherine wasn't swimming. "Too cold for me," she said, shivering. "Ice water." That and other excuses, though she once loved swimming. On oppressively hot days, she might walk in to her knees and let Randy splash her. "Water demon," she calls him then, "you *splashed* your mother!"

"Randy can swim anywhere he likes," Catherine hissed at Matthew after Lucy left. "She doesn't own the water. Who the hell does she think she is?"

. . .

Catherine works her clay into a ball, then hollows it with her thumbs. She works for consistency: no portion of the skull more than half an inch thick. Clay too thick dries unevenly and is apt to crack in the kiln. The apple she made for her fruit series cracked. So did the mango. The grapes turned out O.K. Matthew said they were obviously grapes, ripe Concord grapes—but he often lies to spare her feelings. "Do you really think they look like grapes?"

"Yes!"

"They do not. You lie. I can tell—your ears are red."

"You lie!" he said.

"Sometimes," she said.

. . .

Catherine mounds the clay nose, traces the eyes, scoops nostrils with a fingernail, Lucy's porcine nostrils—and no mistaking them. This will be a decorative head, as real as Cath-

erine can make it with fingers that don't always cooperate.
The numbness comes and goes. Sometimes there are spasms.
Not only in her hands, but in her arms, her back, her legs.
Twice she has fallen when a leg gave out. No pain, just
sudden weakness, and she toppled like a stack of one-too-
many building blocks, surprised to find herself on the floor
looking up.

Some days she feels well enough to run up Mt. Chicorua
and dance on the summit; other days she can barely lift her
feet.

"The best part about moving," she told Matthew, "besides
your marvelous promotion, is getting away from those same
stupid doctors and their stupid, stupid tests. They're quacks —
the bunch of them. I'm not going to listen to any more quacks,
Matthew, except the feathered ones that swim around the
lake."

They'd spotted ducks the day the real-estate agent showed
them the house, a mother and five babies paddling by — a wel-
coming committee, six good omens — small brown ducks,
silent on the water.

"Oh," Catherine said. "Look at them!"

Matthew and Randy's raucous duck calls startled them into
a U-turn. "You silly guys," she said, "you've scared them off,"
struck by the likeness of father and son in silhouette — one tall,
one small, at the water's edge, both quacking optimistically.

·　·　·

Weeks later, they fed the ducks from their own rickety dock.
Randy, legs dangling, tossed broken crackers, crusts of bread.
The same family of brown ducks, could be, the ducklings now
nearly as big as the mother. A brave one sailed under Randy's
feet, nipped his toe, small and white like the bread.

"What did that duck do?" Matthew said.

Randy decided not to cry. He laughed instead. Catherine laughed too, kneeling beside him. She laughed and cried because she was laughing.

"You O.K.?" Matthew said.

"Sure," she said, her throat closing, the air heavy as blankets. She ran for the house.

"What?" Matthew called after her. "What now?"

From the steps, she turned and called back, "Nothing. I'm going in for more bread." Then, angry: "Is that all right with you?"

"Catherine," he said.

"I'm sorry," she said. She couldn't be more sorry. "I'm just tired."

Next day a note appeared in their newspaper box: "Please refrain from feeding ducks near swimming areas, public and private, on our lake. Ducks foul the water. Their excretions cause swimmer's rash." The note was perfectly typed, crisply folded. It smelled faintly of furniture polish.

Catherine knew it was from Lucy. "I hate that woman," she told Matthew.

"You barely know her," he said. "She's just different. You'll get used to her."

"I feel like I've hated her all my life. I hate her hair. I hate her piggy eyes. I hate her pink shirts. I hate her smugness. Don't you hate her?"

"I guess," he said. "I don't know. She doesn't bother me."

"Nothing bothers you!" she said. The words hung between them. Matthew waited. Whatever he said, it would be wrong. He's learned to wait until the flare of anger fades.

It fades.

"I'm sorry," she said. "God, Matthew, she's spoiling everything." *God,* she thought, *I'm spoiling everything.* Her voice cracked. "Never mind," she said, and turned away so he couldn't see her face.

.   .   .

Catherine presses one soft, clay ear firmly into place, then the other, not quite aligned. Clay under her fingernails. Her fingers gray with it. Knuckles stiff with it. Waxy odor of clay drying fast.

The head upside down could be a small bowl or even a vase; on its side, a cornucopia.

.   .   .

At the Lake Association meeting, Catherine felt distinctly uncomfortable. Sidelong glances and suspended conversations suggested the membership had been warned: the new people are difficult, unfriendly, they swim in front of other people's houses, they feed the ducks, they wear big hats, they are not our kind. Lucy would whisper her condemnation. Secret sharing: Look how thin that new woman is. Is she limping? See how her eyes close as though she can barely hold them open. What's wrong with her?

Paranoid, Catherine thought. *Now you're getting paranoid.*

She had wanted Matthew to attend instead: "You go," she said.

"No, you go."

"No, you."

And they had laughed together.

Someone had to stay home with Randy. Someone ought to go. It was a chance to participate. Refreshments would be served. "They can't all be as miserable as Lucy," Matthew said. "It'll be good for you to get out."

"What do you mean by that?" she said.

"Nothing," he said. He looked hurt. She hurts him every day. He doesn't deserve it. Then the black thought: *He and Randy would be better off without me.*

She sat near the back beside a soft-faced, soft-eyed old woman who introduced herself right away—"I'm Marion from North Cove, and you?" Marion had brought her quilting. Catherine watched a saw-tooth star take shape in her hands. She would tell Matthew funny stories about the meeting. She would imitate the Yankee drawls, those soft *a*'s and dropped *r*'s. She would tell him about the chairman's bow tie and presumptuous wink. He winks approval. He winks secret knowledge. He winks. (Maybe it's a tic.) She would describe Lucy, at the head table, scribbling notes, head down, occasionally the head snapping up, a glare at the chairman or the speaker, a disapproving shake of the beige head, and (did Catherine imagine it?) a malevolent sliding of the eyes in Catherine's direction: Lucy looking through her as though she were a pane of glass.

The meeting peaked with an outbreak of ranting about the public beach. "It's a nuisance," someone said. The litter, the noise, kids screeching and screaming, radios blaring. "It's a mess," said the looming man with the handlebar mustache. "The town does nothing. Of course it's polluted. What do you expect?" The mustache quivered, "A hundred people on a Sunday afternoon all peeing in the water."

Marion dropped her quilting, shocked by the news of all that peeing: "Doesn't the town provide proper facilities? Oh, I think they should?"

"Chemical toilet," Lucy croaked. She didn't raise her head, still scribbling; the words rolled out from under her round chin: "One filthy chemical toilet."

Catherine raised her hand to respond. That Lucy! People had a right to swim even if they didn't own lake property, didn't they? What was the membership suggesting—that the public beach be closed altogether? Could they do that?

The chairman tugged on his tie, winked at Catherine, and pointed his gavel. But before she could open her mouth, Lucy said: "Is this a *public* meeting?"

"Well," the chairman said, "if the young lady"—wink—"has something to contribute—"

"Only members speak. She hasn't paid any dues that I know of." Lucy scanned the room for support. She lifted her chin, clamped her lips together, flared her nostrils. "Check your by-laws," she said.

.   .   .

When Lief shuffles up behind her and touches her shoulder, Catherine jumps.

"Sorry," he says. "Hmm—a head. Very nice. Very creative." He bends to inspect her project, his breath musty with the strong coffee he sips all evening long, the mug warming on the wood stove when it's not in his hands, at his lips. Catherine wipes her hands on the dirty towel.

The head looks suddenly crude, lopsided. Randy could have done better.

"It's not quite finished," she says, rounding and re-rounding the chin—seeking the precise angle of intolerance.

Lief asks should the head have hair, or is this a bald person?

"Oh yes," she says, "this girl has hair." With a needle, she carves hair into the skull: slender, curving lines that suggest fine unruffled, unrufflable hair. She carves points at the ears: tender ears, wide-lobed, pressed close to the curve of skull, closer. She builds ear folds with clay worms. She digs tiny canals.

"Fancy," Lief says.

She looks up to see if he's teasing. He's not. His face is solemn as stone.

. . .

Eventually, Lucy got to Matthew, too: Matthew the tolerant, whose motto to this point had been let's-at-least-try-to-get-along; Matthew who believed that all problems had solutions, even a next-door neighbor like Lucy Dahl.

"What about that new float rope out in front of *her* house," he snapped at the building inspector. It took a lot to make Matthew mad. Lucy had managed. His dark eyes widened. He waved his arms in an arc of frustration. "Doesn't she need a permit for that?"

"Anything on the water, that's state jurisdiction," the inspector said, tight-lipped. "Nothing to do with me." He sniffed.

"It's a grudge rope," Matthew said. "You've heard of a grudge fence—well, that's a grudge rope. That woman—"

"Nothing to do with me." Sniff. "State jurisdiction."

Catherine asked who had lodged the complaint in the first place—the unfounded complaint that she and Matthew were renovating the house without proper permits.

"I might have driven by myself and noticed the new railing or the pile of lumber," the inspector said.

"But you didn't," Catherine said, "did you."

. . .

Catherine leans back for a new angle on the head protruding from the tabletop.

"After you dry, I'll paint you," she says.

Lief, at the wheel trying to save another student's too-tall vase from collapse, tilts his head as though he's listening, nods as though he heard what she said. She thought he and the others were out of range. She hoped they were. This is between her and the head of her enemy.

"Then I will dip you," she whispers. "Then I will drown you in a glaze of crushed glass."

. . .

Catherine digs out her old bathing suit and slips it on. The elastic is loose around the legs and the front hangs a little, as though it is not her suit at all, but the property of some other, larger, woman.

In the mirror she sees herself as others might—long-necked and bony-shouldered, with twigs for arms. (Last night when she undressed for bed, Matthew said, "You look fine. You look great. Better than ever." *Sweet, miserable liar.*) She looks as though she'd have trouble lifting a grocery bag. She looks as though she'd have trouble walking up a flight of stairs. She looks sickly thin. But she feels strong. She feels, at this moment, as strong as ever.

She lifts the twigs over her head and turns. Her stomach is as flat as when she was a teenager.

On the porch, she straps on the flippers and flip-flops sideways down the steps. She doesn't hold the rail. Matthew says, "I'll come with you. Just give me a minute to change."

"I'll be fine," she says. "I'll swim just off-shore, no deeper than my armpits—right, Randy, that's the rule."

"I want to come," Randy says. "I'm real hot."

Matthew looks sheepish, as though he's about to say something trite and sentimental. She braces herself.

Instead he says: "You look like a duck."

Yellow suit, black flippers: "I am a duck." She waddles toward the water. She quacks provocatively.

In the end, they all go. The water is warm from the heat of the day, from the accumulated heat of the season. Afternoon meets evening, the sun low, sinking into the lake. Windows in the houses along the east shore reflect the long rays like golden eyes. The lake shimmers. This could be the last hot day of the season, the last chance for swimming.

They swim the red-and-white perimeter of Lucy Dahl's float rope. Catherine wants to swim not just in circles, but somewhere. Somewhere. They head down shore toward the infamous public beach, agreeing to take their time, agreeing that if anybody gets tired, they'll turn back, knowing they will not turn back. "Don't push it," Matthew says.

"Don't worry," she says. "I need for you to stop worrying."

"Since when am I worried."

"Since lately," she says. "My fault."

"Not your fault," he says.

My fault, she thinks.

They swim circles around Randy and Puff. Matthew scrapes an underwater boulder with his knee—about a hundred yards out from shore, and directly in front of Lucy's picture window—a mirror for the sun: Lucy's golden eye.

The water around the boulder is deep enough for diving. Matthew shows off, stretching his arms long over his head, hands together, back and legs straight; a little push-off and he curls like an Olympian into the water.

"Watch this!" Catherine waddles off the edge, holding her nose.

Randy stands on the boulder, pretending to be tall.

Matthew turns into a shark. Randy flails and screeches when the shark grabs his ankle. He and Puff make a miraculous escape, but the shark continues to stalk them just beneath the surface.

Catherine floats on her back, moving her hands for a slow,

smooth propulsion, moving her feet in a slow-motion scissors kick. She floats away from Randy and Matthew, away out deep, away toward the middle of the lake—far enough for privacy, close enough for safety. Not to worry, Matthew. She lets her hair spread over the water and tips her head back to submerge her ears. The quiet comes on strong. Randy and Matthew's voices are reduced to vibrations.

She thinks of Lucy: Lucy behind the reflective window. An enemy watching.

The water feels wonderful, soft and cool all over. The sun warms Catherine's face.

In all her life, she has never met anyone like Lucy Dahl who spits self-righteousness like a venom to which Catherine is particularly susceptible. And here they are neighbors—with the potential to make each other eternally miserable. Catherine knows about misery. In the last few months she has embraced it.

But last night . . . last night she brought the head home from pottery class.

Matthew and Randy stared at it. "It's Lucy Dahl," she told them. "Our neighbor."

"Is it a present?" Matthew said. "A peace offering?"

"No," she said. "It's not for her. It's for me."

"Oh," Matthew said.

"Do you think I caught her essence?"

"It's nice," Matthew said. He hefted it. "Heavy. Heavier than it looks."

"I was so mad," she said. "She made me so mad. Does this make sense? I recreated her. She's going to live on the mantle. She'll like it there."

"She'll look good on the mantle," he said. He placed the head in her hands. His hands over her hands cupping the head. "We love you, you know."

"I know," she said.

Randy liked the head, too. He touched the eyeball. He stuck his nose in the ear and his fingers up the hollow neck. "I want to hold it," he said. "Can I hold it?"

Catherine loves the head. Painted and dipped, with its streaked hair, hard blue eyes (pupils not quite symmetrical), hard red lips, slightly parted as though about to pronounce judgment ("check your bylaws"), it makes her laugh the kind of laugh that doesn't end in a sob. She'd almost forgotten how to laugh that way. She rolled the head along her forearm. Heavy, contoured. She pressed it to her cheek. Cool, smooth.

She can't look at the head without laughing. She can't think of it without smiling. She thinks of it now, and smiles up at the sky. So delicate is the relationship between her body and the water, just that slight stretch of her lips seems to push the back of her head deeper. Maybe the new doctor is right; maybe the choice really is hers.

Weightless and pain-free, she extends her arms. She lets them bob with the motion of small waves. She floats in a universe that laps reassuringly against her. And when she closes her eyes, she is suspended in a perfect darkness. Her heavy legs sink below the sun-warmed surface into the surprise of cold, spring-fed depths.

⚏ Lindy Lowe at Bat

Lindy Lowe, at the plate, is mad.

One strike has been called on her—unfairly. Low and outside, it was not a strike. Either the umpire has bad eyesight or he's cheating.

She shivers. The anemic sun that had warmed them at the start of the game has disappeared in clouds. She hears thunder in the distance. She adjusts her safety goggles, raises her bat high over her shoulder, points her toe, sticks her butt out, and glares at that boob of a Beaumont pitcher looming on the mound like big-time, big-league, I'll strike you out or knock you down, take your choice, little girl.

But Lindy knows she has the power to drive Brian Millitello around the bases. If that Beaumont pitcher gets the ball anywhere near the plate, she'll give it a good ride. She'll follow it all the way in, *all* the way in. And she'll smack it *all* the way out.

Coach, meanwhile, in the dugout tries to ignore his ex-girlfriend, Tina, posing beside the Beaumont cheering section—cheering for Beaumont she'll *say* because her weaselly nephews play. Her cheeks are red from a rouge overdose. Her new perm frizzes in the cool humidity of rain on the way. Her purple scarf, knotted at the neck, makes an inverted V over her right breast.

She hates baseball. She loathes her sassy nephews. Coach knows she is here for one reason only: to torment him.

Hard-eyed Marcia is solemn on the dugout steps; straight, waist-length hair fans over her shoulders and down her back. She folds her arms tight over the scorebook and takes in the whole sorry situation: a glance across the way at Tina, a glance sidelong at Coach, a jut of her chin in Tina's direction as if to say, "What's *she* doing here?" Marcia is hot for Coach, but he doesn't know it and she won't admit it.

Chilled, Coach reaches behind the bench for his crumpled sweatshirt. Tina screams, "Go Beaumont." When she claps, she undulates. Coach focuses on Lindy Lowe, who has the power to advance Brian Millitello and place herself in scoring position: she's thin as a stick, but strong as an alder. She wants to play good ball; Coach wants to teach her. Simple—the way relationships should be. He calls to her and she hears his voice rising over the others: "Settle down, Lindy. Choke up."

Lindy thinks he is the best coach in the world. He hardly ever yells except when they do something really stupid like forget to tag up on a fly ball. But he doesn't lie to them either. Sometimes he says: "You looked good out there. You lost, but you looked good." Sometimes he says, "*That* was a pathetic display. If you can't do better than that we might as well pack up and go home right now."

Early in the season Lindy was hitting well and Coach was pleased. Her specialty was the low power-slug that found the hole in the infield, dropped in for an easy single, an occasional sliding double. Marcia, also known as Little Clay's Mom, said Lindy had the third-highest batting average and if Jason and Brian didn't watch out, she was going to zoom right by them.

After that, though, she came up against some bad pitching, got smacked a couple of times, backed off the base, started anticipating too much, trying too hard. When her average began to slide, her confidence went with it.

Her dad maintains it was just her eyesight that went and the new glasses will make all the difference. "Helps if you can see the ball," he told Coach. "Poor kid's been swinging at ghosts all summer."

Tina reaches for the soda somebody holds out to her from the top of the Beaumont bleachers. Her T-shirt rides up. She puts the red can to her red lips. "If you *really* loved me," she used to tell Coach, "you wouldn't be so crazy jealous." Which made no sense at all to Coach when she parked on his cousin Nate's lap and twined herself around Nate's neck, tickling his pits. Some jerk takes a Polaroid picture, the chair falls over, and the two of them are in a tangle on the floor, laughing like drunks. In the end, what drove Coach away was her if-you-really-loved-me song, and the way she used Nate, but mostly the way she changed the rules as they went along so he couldn't possibly win.

Coach likes to win.

Marcia says Tina's a loser and always has been.

The Beaumont pitcher—a long-bodied, short-legged boy, with the tight-muscled arms of a wrestler—is trying to stare Lindy down, but she stares back the way Coach taught her, the way she might stare at a mosquito sucking blood from her forearm—just before she smacks it.

Brian Millitello takes a healthy lead off first base. He's fast, unpredictable, cocky. He's bouncing on the balls of his feet. Coach signals: Don't take chances; wait for a break. Brian, wild-eyed, stops bouncing for three beats as he absorbs the message. "Hey, Pitch," he taunts. "Hey, hey, Pitch." He flaps his arms and smiles like a demon.

"Come on, Lindy," Coach says. "You can do it." The team takes its cue: WHACK IT, LINDY, WHACK IT OVER THE FENCE JUST LIKE ENFIELD—OUTTA THE PARK, LINDY—JUST LIKE YOU AL-WAYS DO.

She appreciates the beautiful lie. She has never whacked

one over the fence—not in Enfield, not in Avery, not anywhere. She hasn't even connected with the ball, except to foul,
in the last three games. But her new glasses make the ball look
big—big as a cantaloupe hurtling toward her, big enough to
hit with a broom handle. She's not afraid of the burly pitcher
with the wicked fast ball that, in previous at-bats, blew her away
from the plate, heart pounding because she knows what it feels
like to be hit with a wicked fast ball in the side or the hip or
the thigh. The ball-sized black and blue on her rear end is a
souvenir of batting practice opposite James Schlitz—their own
wild fast-ball pitcher. "James has the arm," Coach says, "if he
could just control it." Lindy's butt agrees.

The pitcher winds up. Lindy stiffens. Her grip is firm and
steady. The pitcher fires. Her eye is on the ball *all* the way in.
She twitches, but does not reach. The ball slides by, nose-high
and outside.

"Steeeee-rike," yells the umpire.

Lindy whirls to face him: "Strike?"

The umpire tries to shrink her with a watery stare. His jaw
is set and the color high in his pockmarked cheeks. But Lindy
is unshrinkable. She stares back. The catcher smirks under
his mask. "Strike," he hisses, just loud enough for Lindy
to hear.

She turns to the dugout for support. Coach emerges into the
mist along the foul line, scowling, hands deep in the pouch of
his sweatshirt. He blows, like a whale, a gust of frustration.

Lindy pantomimes "Strike?"—all teeth—afraid to say it
aloud again; she's been warned to hold back around umpires.
They're touchy.

Her dad says he got thrown out of a game when he was a
kid—for spitting on the umpire's shoe. She understands the
impulse, and she knows how dramatic Old Dad gets when his
temper kicks in.

"That's all right, honey," she hears him boom from the bleachers—on the verge of dramatics. "Good eye!"

"That's all right, Lindy," Marcia yells, "it just takes one." Little Clay is on deck, so Marcia is excited. She gets that way when her boy comes up to bat. Sometimes it's so bad she forgets to mark the score in the book. They'll say: "What's the score, what's the score, Marcia?" She'll say: "Don't worry about the score. You just play ball and I'll worry about the score."

Lindy thinks the reason Marcia helps out (besides wanting to be around Coach) is so she can watch after Little Clay, make sure he doesn't get hurt, make sure he doesn't get his feelings hurt when he messes up—which he usually does. Earlier in the game Little Clay's dad—Big Clay—showed up. Drunk. Lindy knows drunk when she sees it. He walked light and un- steady as though he didn't quite know where his feet were. He and Coach almost got into a fight when Coach signaled for a steal with two outs and Jason got picked off at third. Big Clay said that was a stupid move.

Coach said: "If you want to run this team, Mister, you come over here and run it. Otherwise, shut your mouth."

"This is a public park," Big Clay said. "I'll say what I want to say to who I . . . who I want to say it to if I want to. I got as much right to be here as anybody else."

But Marcia said he had to stay away from them (because of the restraining order). She said she'd call the police if he didn't get out. Now. He backed off. "I got an appointment anyway. Things to do. I can't stand to watch this figgin' . . . friggin' . . . farce," he said. On the way out, he slipped on the grass and rolled down the bank onto the tar of the parking lot. His friend picked him up and maneuvered him into the passenger side of the truck. Little Clay put his head down and studied the webbing on his glove. To make him feel better, all the kids pretended they hadn't noticed his dad at all. The game went on. Pretty soon Clay lifted his head. Pretty soon he was chattering along with the rest of them. Lindy looked closely at his eyes. They were red.

Clay is the second-worst player on the team. In the field he's slow, he often misjudges grounders, and he inevitably hesitates before the throw. At bat, he goes for sucker balls—high and too far outside or, sometimes, bouncing off the plate. When he does connect though . . . pow! This is what makes him better than the worst player, who's littler, scared of the ball, and only nine: Clay's ability to, on occasion, hit a home run. A plump boy with a soft freckled face, Little Clay brags sometimes, but nobody minds: "Did you see that? Did you see me hit that good one? That was a wicked good hit, wasn't it?"

If Lindy gets on base, it'll be up to him to hit her in. On deck, he taps his favorite aluminum bat against the sides of his cleats to knock the dirt out.

"Settle down, Lindy," Coach says. "This is your ball. You own this ball. Take your time." He offers a small, cool smile that means: pay those cheaters back the only way it really counts —with a hit. The smile curls the wisp of mustache on his lip. Lindy thinks he's almost as handsome as her dad. She nods back, determined: *I understand, Coach; I will not let you down.*

But she has run short of choices. Unless she gets smacked by the pitch and takes a base that way, her only option is to swing at whatever comes down the pike. This umpire sees nothing but strikes, so a walk is out of the question. If she has to reach, she'll reach. If she has to leap over the base or into the air or scrunch like a squirrel to connect, she is prepared to do so.

A third called strike in a game this important and this close is a humiliation Lindy Lowe is unwilling to bear. If she has to go down, she'll go down swinging. She will spit in the face of injustice. She will, at the very least, spit in her palm when it's time to line up and shake hands with the other team. She will spit fresh when she sees that smirking catcher coming her way. She scrapes her feet vigorously on the damp earth, hoping to splat him with a clod as he squats behind her.

She is worried though. A glance at the bleachers reveals her dad's death grip on the seat; he's leaning forward, his chest just about touching his knees. He looks like a spring about to be sprung and he hasn't been feeling good—the sweat breaks out and his face gets tight and pale. It's not good for him to lose his temper and get dramatic anymore. Doctor said so.

She shakes her hair out of her eyes, sniffs and blinks hard to focus. A hit at this point could avert any number of disasters.

She hears her dad call: "Choke up. Choke up, Lindy. Nice level swing." He's about two turns short of hurtling off the bleachers, telling that strike-happy umpire what he thinks of his attitude and eyesight. God knows what will happen if the umpire makes the mistake of trying to defend himself. Her dad, once his temper's lit, is apt to spark like Fourth of July.

The team yells: KILL IT, LINDY, KILL IT. OUT OF THE PARK, LINDY. JUST LIKE LAST TIME.

Right. Just like last time. Listening to them, she can almost believe there was a last time. The pitcher believes she can hit the ball. Something in her stance, in the tilt of her chin, in the lift of the bat tells him so.

The voices fade. Lindy feels the smooth, curved wood in her hands, the mist on her face. She and the burly Beaumont pitcher are alone, transfixed in a naked staredown. Everything fades except the dark holes that are her opponent's eyes.

Come on, Pitcher. Fire it in here. I am ready.

She takes a deep, steadying breath.

Ready.

But Brian Millitello—the speed demon on first base—sees his chance and takes it. He breaks for second, a full-speed torpedo in cleats, out of the chute and no turning back. Coach screams a long hoarse "Go!"

The pitcher twists, throws.

Lindy steps away from the plate.

Brian slides, belly down, fingers reaching. He touches the bag. The ball slaps the second baseman's glove.

The team screams, "YES."

"OUT," yells the base umpire.

"OUT?" yell the parents in the bleachers. "OUT?" Old Dad wails, leaping to his feet. She hopes he's got his pills with him. Mr. Schlitz, on the bleachers behind, grabs him by the shoulders, holds him back. They hold each other back. Marcia presses her lips together and pushes at her hair. Coach's head drops to his chest. His eyes close. Slowly, he opens them—but the nightmare persists. Brian is still out. Lindy stands quiet, stunned.

Coach and the plate umpire stalk to second base. Coach points at the bag. He points at Brian who is brushing himself off, wild-eyed. He'd waited for his moment, just like Coach said. He'd run hard. He'd slid perfectly. He was safe!

"I was safe," Brian says, keeping one foot on the bag, just in case the umpire comes to his senses and reverses his decision. "Shut up," Coach says. "I'll handle this." Brian shuts up. He's going nowhere until Coach tells him to. They'll have to pry him off this base like a bloodsucker from a swimmer's calf. They'll have to burn him off with giant matches. They'll have to sprinkle ten pounds of salt on his head.

From the dugout the team protests, agonized. "Shut up," Marcia says. The protest diminishes to a collective sob, a quiet moan. Marcia blocks the exit with her body, a plug in the zing hole of a hornet's nest: they are subdued now, but for how long? Her mission, a mother's mission: keep the kids out of the fray. She watches Coach and the umpires in their nose-to-nose exchange. She can't hear a word of it, but she is transfixed by the passion shimmering in the air around them. Or is it the beginning of the rain—the drops almost too fine to detect.

Tina's face, suddenly, fills Marcia's field of vision. Tina is bigger than life and stinking of drug-store cologne. Marcia steps to the side to see around her. Tina steps that way too. They are dancing the two-step. Marcia catches at the dugout post to hold her position on the edge of the stairs.

Tina says: "If I want him back, I'll get him back."

Marcia says: "What *is* your problem?"

Tina says: "You're going to be the one with the problem if you keep it up. I'm embarrassed for you. You're at least five years older than him for one thing."

Marcia says: "Do you want to eat this scorebook?"

Meanwhile, the confrontation at second base escalates. The arrogant Beaumont coach, his belly girdled by the tight polyester uniform, thrusts himself into the huddle. Coach—slight and intense, his hands fisted at his sides—talks fast, face flushing.

It starts to rain. Marcia, in the shelter of the dugout overhang, stays dry. Tina gets hit with both the rain and the runoff. Her perm flattens like tissue paper. Water catches on her lashes, pools there momentarily, then her mascara starts to run in hideous black rivulets down her face. Her chin drips black. Her purple scarf will soon be bleeding into her T-shirt.

Lindy worries that the rain will ruin her baseball hat: there's a waterfall flowing over the bill. Should she run for shelter or stay put between the on-deck box and the plate? She and Little Clay look at each other and shrug; they move closer together. They stay put, side by side, hats dripping.

The deluge breaks up the huddle at second base. Coach puts his hand on Brian Millitello's head and they stalk together off the field—Brian stalking twice as fast as Coach, just to keep up. The thunder comes again. Closer now. Close enough to startle people.

"Are they going to call it?" Lindy's dad yells from the bleachers, a newspaper tented over his head. The others have run for their cars but Old Dad doesn't budge. His girl is still at bat.

"No way!" Coach says. "Lindy—get ready. We're going to finish our ups if we have to swim the bases."

Old Dad says, "Ya, but . . ."

Coach says, "I told them we're going to finish our ups. That's it."

Lindy believes him.

Marcia has draped herself in a plastic poncho—just the bill of her cap and the tip of her nose exposed. She stands beside Coach at the baseline. "There's three kids crying in the dugout," she says.

"We're not going home," he says, "until we turn this thing around."

She says, "They're pretty discouraged—they think we're getting knocked out of the playoffs because of cheating."

Coach says, "No way!" And as he says it, the downpour lets up a little—it's a drizzle, it's a shower, it's nothing to be concerned about, certainly nothing to call a game on account of. Marcia pictures Tina, drowned ratty, huddling in her car, waiting for Coach to come to her so she can hurt him again. But she won't. Marcia will make sure of that.

Coach says, "TEAM! Talk it up—talk it up! All it takes is one."

Lindy steps into the batter's box.

GO LINDY—SHOW 'EM WHAT YOU CAN DO—OUTTA THE PARK, LIN-DY.

Little Clay, in the on-deck box, takes warm-up swings so vigorous there appears to be some danger he'll hit himself in the head on the follow-through. "Good cut, Clay," Coach says over a rumble of thunder, a thin, distant flash of lightning, "but don't use the aluminum bat," tossing him a wooden one.

Marcia whispers in Coach's ear: "Did you see Tina over here, causing trouble?"

"I didn't notice," he says.

Marcia smiles.

Coach claps his hands three times. The team picks up the rhythm, increases its chatter—the hive is humming.

Lindy adjusts her safety goggles, raises her good old wooden bat high over her shoulder, points her toe, sticks her butt out. The tip of the bat makes small menacing circles in the air.

"One good pitch," the Beaumont coach yells. "Strike her out, Don-Don. Strike her out and we're out of here."

Lindy's dad disentangles himself from the wet newspaper. He yells: "HIT IT." The crack of the bat making solid contact with a not-so-wicked fast ball punctuates the sentiment and Lindy, always light on her feet, is hydroplaning toward first base.

Don-Don, having lost his balance on the wet mound, is down, trying to find his feet when the ball whizzes over his head. He reaches—but too late.

Old Dad says, reverently: "Line drive."

Lindy rounds first, heads for second. The center fielder, who underestimated her power, has to run back for the ball which is rolling away from him toward the fence but stops just short. He gets a glove on it, grips it with his throwing hand, hesitates: Where's the play?

Someone screams second.

Lindy runs full speed, focused on the base ahead, conscious only of the power of her muscles, the strength of her bones. She pumps as hard as she can. She doesn't look for where the ball has gone, or who has it, or where it is going. She doesn't look at Coach for a green light or a red light. She doesn't look at anybody—she just goes.

No one knows it yet (except possibly Old Dad, from whom she inherited a good deal of her spirit and bull-headedness), but the moment bat connected with ball, Lindy Lowe made up her mind to run the bases. All of them. Full out. Non-stop. Whatever the consequences.

The center fielder, a logical boy, throws to second. But Lindy blows by the second baseman long before the lobbed ball arrives. And the second baseman, watching Lindy run, is forced to hop out of her way or be barreled over. He throws his glove up too late—the ball rolls out of it, onto the ground.

He can't see. The ball is muddy, there's water in his eyes —he feels around, knocking the ball a few feet down the base-line. He dives, throws from his knees to some phantom player standing halfway between the third baseman and the short stop.

By then Lindy has already whizzed by third and is on her way home.

As the ball slides into foul territory, with three humiliated Beaumont players hot on its trail, Lindy slides home. She is jumping up and down on the puddle that used to be home plate and the team is rushing out to greet her. Little Clay gets there first. They high-five and he says, "I'm gonna hit a good one. You're gonna see me hit a home run now. Everybody's gonna see."

And Little Clay is right. The rally has begun.

⚎ Minna Runs for Selectman

When I mention small potatoes, I'm certainly not referring to my opponent's manly parts. Though it seems as though he thinks so, the way he reacts—red above his collar, veins pulsing in neck and temple, hands gripping the lectern.

His hair is tousled on the sides but the blond toupee across his forehead is as slick as a flattened gerbil.

There is a long silence.

I breathe heavily into the microphone, focusing on Amos Clark, chairman of the budget committee, who leans like a willow against the great oak doors at the back. If some latecomer opens those doors quick, Amos Clark will topple.

This image sustains me.

It is hard, you know, to stand before a room jam-packed with neighbors, acquaintances, friends, enemies, strangers—and tell the truth. It is hard with the heat rising from bodies elbow to elbow on folding chairs and benches, the crowd spilling out into the corridor by the tax collector's office. It is hard to express, in a strong voice, versions of the truth bound to make people mad.

"Yes," I say, "you might not think much of that fancy fifteen-button telephone and that plush carpet in *your* office and the thirty-percent raise for the so-called Administrative Assistant who also happens to be . . . your mother-in-law!"

Franklin's head snaps around at that. He begins to shape a response—I can sense it rising, from his bowels through the cavern of his stomach along his constricted gorge to that place behind his teeth where, among civilized persons, the visceral pauses, awaiting clearance. He is a civilized person after all. And so am I. And so are we all.

I want to say: Franklin, it is not, in fact, the telephone or the carpet or your mother-in-law I really object to. They are just easy targets. What I *really* object to is your lack of vision, your laziness, your selfishness, your arrogance. What I really object to is you.

But to say this would be to cross the line: too direct, too hurtful, too true. A personal attack, they'd say.

Dear God, I say, is there any other kind worth making?

I press on: "You may consider these items *small potatoes* in light of the whole town budget—but they add up, you know. With all due respect, they add up, Franklin."

A smattering of applause from the Constitutional Fundamentalists (an extended family of Gooches on the bench by the windows—Grandma Gooch, Grampa Gooch, the Gooch twins, their wives, ex-wives, cousins, and off-spring).

"Yeah," yells a Gooch, "how's the old people supposed to live, huh?"

I smile upon the Gooches, who are in the process of suing the planning board for their constitutional right to raise pigs along Main Street. They are not my preferred constituency, but support from any quarter is welcome. My husband and campaign staff (those who colored in posters, planted "Minna's a Winna" signs at intersections, addressed envelopes and licked stamps for the mail blitz) sit quietly in the fourth row studying their crotches. Darcy blows her tiny nose. Gloria reaches into her pocketbook for lifesavers—wintergreen, for its calming effect. She is nervous. They are all nervous. They think I've gone too far with the mother-in-law crack. They are worried that in the heat of the moment I will go further still. And it's true, I'm just warming up.

. . .

My husband, Brian, didn't want me to run. He thought I'd melt from the publicity and criticism. He thought I'd crack, fold, blister, and sustain general psychological damage. Also, there was the question of business. Would townsfolk continue to buy Farm Fair insurance from a man whose wife was a political lightning rod?

"We still have to live in this town," he said. "When all is said and done, we still have to live in this town. Remember that, Minna."

For a while, it looked as though Franklin Pilsnor would be running unopposed. But every day at the P.O., at the grocery store, at the library, at the gas station, every day somebody was saying: "That knucklehead's done nothing for this town. He's done nothing but line his own pockets. He's a snotty little so-and-so who got elected on the Pilsnor name—somebody's got to stand up to him." Or words to that effect.

So I thought: Why not me?

I knew a lot of voters through PTA as well as the Quilting and Good Works Club of which I've been recording secretary since 1975. Gloria told me I should run. She said a lot of people thought the same. "I want to make a difference," I told Brian. "Does that sound stupid?"

"Yes," he said. "It is stupid. If you lose you lose and if you win you lose because being selectman is a miserable, thankless—"

"Selectdud," I said, sounding like my dear-little-feminist daughter. "Please use the sex-neutral term."

"If you stick your neck out, somebody's going to step on it," he said. "Why don't you do aerobics, take a course, adopt a dog, get a job."

I don't want to do aerobics. I'm sick of taking courses. I hate dogs, especially since ours disappeared. (Gloria says Buster was probably shot chasing deer—but I don't believe it. I'm still expecting to hear him scratch at the back door. I hate dogs because they leave without warning.) And I have a job. Fifteen hours a week at the Avery Lending Library—shelving books, typing cards, stamping flaps, and so forth. He knows that.

But I shut my mouth on the subject and so does he. This is the way things often end between us now that our daughter has left us for college: Quietly. As though fighting is no longer worth the effort.

.   .   .

The moderator recognizes Franklin's mother-in-law. She is a fairy-tale witch in maroon polyester: short, pasty, hunched. Her eyes glitter behind thick glasses. She is a force to be reckoned with. As am I.

She opens her mouth to speak but a Gooch yells, "Use the microphone."

The moderator, a plump young man who is also part-time pastor of the Congregational Church, says: "Please use the microphone so everyone can hear."

So Grace Kingsbury, administrative assistant to the selectmen, stumbles toward the center aisle. She is sitting in a fat man's lap. She is doubled over the knees of the teenager next to him who tries to rise. She is choking on somebody's Old Spice. She is finally out, squeezing her foot back into the shoe that popped loose. She steps up to the microphone, which is just about level with her forehead, adjusts the stand for height. She curls her hand protectively over the top button of her cardigan.

I search for Brian's eyes in the fourth row, but they are miss-

ing and so is the rest of him. The chair beside Gloria is conspic-
uously empty. He has skipped home to watch the Celtics. He
said he would and he did.

Grace Kingsbury raves about tradition, public service, family history. She wallows in the "we." We, we, we: the Kings-
burys, the Pilsnors; oh, what *we* have done for *our* town. "She,"
on the other hand, meaning me, is *not even a native*.

"Isn't it true, Madame Candidate," she says, "that not only
did I receive a promotion but also increased hours? I am working more hours at a different job so, of course, I am entitled to
a higher rate of pay. Why don't you tell these people the whole
story, Minna?"

Applause from the crowd—from the fire-department crowd
in the back, from the Avery Amateur Theater crowd to the left,
from the town-hall employees contingent shoulder to shoulder
in the hallway, applause even from a couple of rogue Gooches.

Franklin, shaded by his toupee, pretends to study the note
cards on his lectern, aligning and realigning them with long
pale hands as though about to perform a card trick. He is
smirking.

I hate smirking.

"We're paying out thirty percent more on that line this year
than last," I say. "And, you know, the service isn't any better. I
still had to wait half an hour to collect my dump sticker. Grace,
you're available to the public only four hours a day, three days
a week at remarkably inconvenient times. As for the selectmen—I don't know when they're available, are they ever?
Franklin, I'm asking you."

"Franklin didn't even vote on me!" Grace squawks. "He ab-
stained. It was the other two. And it wasn't thirty percent, it was
twenty-eight point five. Get your facts straight, sweetheart."

I do not squawk. Instead I say in my low, steady, dangerous
voice: "My facts are straight, sweetheart. I rounded off."

. . .

Gloria says small-town politics are the last of the blood sports. We share a quiet moment in the parking lot of town hall yard, empty now except for the two of us and a circle of smokers lingering in the yellow light of the open door.

It is dark—clouds obscure the moon, a fog rises and swirls in a breeze chilled by the last of the melting snow. Gloria and I stand just outside the light from the lampposts along the bricked walkway. Behind us a ground beacon glares up at the American flag which flaps like a giant bat.

She presses lifesavers into my hand. I am hot inside and cold outside like I'm coming down with something, probably Darcy's cold which will turn into the flu which will turn into pneumonia and then I'll die and then they'll be sorry. I peel away the foil.

We hear laughter from the smokers. I think they are laughing at me.

"I think it went well," she says. "I think people could see you were sincere and not an idiot like Franklin and not a bitch like Grace Kingsbury."

"My motivations are pure," I say, believing it.

I do not say, but this is what I think late at night when I can't sleep for wondering why: I am running because Franklin Pilsnor is a self-serving manipulator and the other two select-duds are Gumbys in his hands. I am running because this town is caught in a web of questionable traditions and inefficiencies justified by: "This is the way it's always been done." I am running for the good of my community.

But to this noble end I engaged in an ignoble public confrontation—something Gloria herself would never do. Her style is to smile at enemies through clenched teeth, to ask how the garden grows while murmuring gypsy curses. Maybe she

should be the candidate and I should be her campaign manager. Maybe subtlety and tact *are* political assets after all.

"Franklin is an idiot," she says. "He looks like an idiot. He
talks like an idiot. Anyone in the audience who was not an idiot
could see that clearly."

All I can see of her in this peculiar misty darkness is shadow
and the gleam of her teeth and the glint of her dangle earrings.
"You told the truth," she says. "Who can fault you for that?"

"Idiots," I say.

·   ·   ·

Two days after the debate and one day before the election, I
walk into the house and hear Brian on the phone with Susan:
"Are you eating? Are you behaving yourself?"

Questions for the child she is no longer.

I hear him say: "Your mother's up to her neck in it."

I hear him say: "That's what worries me. I'm afraid she will
win." He laughs. They are laughing together. I feel the feather
touch of isolation.

When he hangs up I am standing right behind him, pulsing
with a sledge-hammer of a headache that has struck without
warning. I notice, from this close range, how gray his hair has
become, how badly it needs trimming. I notice two new moles
on the back of his neck. I notice he is a stranger. I say, in my
low, steady, dangerous voice, "You know, I might have enjoyed
talking with her."

He turns, startled. "I didn't even know you were back," he
says. "I didn't even know you were in the house."

We are in the kitchen, my favorite room, the room in which
on dreary days, I used to drink tea late afternoons reading my
magazines in front of a small fire with the dog at my feet. Since
the campaign, I have no time for tea or reading or a fire, and,
of course, the dog is missing.

I turn my back on my husband, stalk to the tall cupboard and reach for the McCoy teapot, one among fourteen sister teapots displayed on the top shelf, a shelf so high I have to rise on tiptoe and stretch my arm its full length to grasp the handle. The teapot was my gift from Brian last Christmas. White with large brown and blue flowers, it is a squat, ugly teapot.

"Is something wrong?" he says.

I note, through a haze, that my kitchen is a mess: the dishes undone, the floor unswept, the table littered with the remnants of Brian's supper and (is that egg grease I see?) his breakfast as well. I would like to have tea, yes I would, but find no space on my table or my counter uncluttered enough to set the pot.

Tomorrow I will stand for hours in front of town hall promoting my candidacy, acting like a reasonable person, a person for whom another reasonable person could, in good conscience, vote. Tonight I do not feel particularly reasonable.

I lift the lid from the McCoy. In my cold hand, it is round and smooth. I drop it on the floor. It doesn't break. I pick it up and hurl it at the hearth. It strikes just below and slightly to the left of the Dutch oven. The lid breaks. Then I drop the pot. It breaks too, with the marvelous chalky sound of clay on inlaid linoleum.

"Stop it," Brian says. He steps forward as though to restrain me; the clay scrunches under his feet. "Don't touch me," I say. "I like to break teapots. I like the way they sound when they break. I think I'm going to break some more."

"What's wrong," he says. I grab a kitchen chair and shove it toward the tall cupboard. I jump up on the chair. Now I tower over him. Now the teapots are all easily within reach.

.   .   .

When the dust clears, Brian is standing in the shelter of the refrigerator with his hands in his pockets and a pained look on his face. I am sweeping broken teapots—not only the McCoy but two Halls and an Occupied Japan. "I want the dishes to be washed," I say. "I want tomorrow to be over!"

He squirts detergent into the sink and runs the hot water while I sweep. I dump the wreckage into a brown grocery bag and carry the grocery bag to the galvanized barrel on the porch.

When I come back in he puts his arms around me. I can smell his soapy hands. I miss my teapots already.

He says, "You are a good person, Minna."

Over his shoulder I see there are a few teapots left on the shelf. One is my favorite—a six-cupper, the surface ridged to suggest basket weave, a basket full of roses. This teapot came to me from my grandmother Dix. I spared it. Even in my rage, I exerted enough self-control to spare my grandmother's wonderful teapot.

I *am* a good person.

It's supposed to rain tomorrow. Gloria and I, maybe Darcy, will take turns outside the polls accosting voters. We will press damp flyers into their hands. We will smile, make pleasant, conservative remarks.

"You are going to vote for me," I say, after the kitchen is cleaned and the tea poured, steaming. "Brian? You *are* going to vote for me."

. . .

When Amos Clark approaches at the official counting of the ballots, I think he's maybe going to speak of his support or wish me luck or advise me about how to handle myself in the exalted office of selectman should an upset victory occur.

Long, lanky, smelling ever-so-slightly of the sheep he raises with his wife, the weaver, he straddles a chair in front of me.

His wife stands directly behind him, hands folded over her stomach. A hand-woven poncho, in several shades of red, reaches to her knees. As simple and inoffensive as a wilted strawberry, she smiles. I have been smiling all day myself, having stopped about two hours ago when the polls closed, when there were no votes left to win. Her smile is lopsided and empty. Across the room, Franklin Pilsnor's toupee gleams in the harsh fluorescent light. He is circling, circulating.

"Neck and neck," Amos says, "sounds like to me."

I shrug modestly. Listening to the count I hear my name; I hear Pilsnor's; I hear lots of names because there are many offices to be filled; I hear, regarding the incumbent running uncontested for school board, "Anybody but him."

We spectators are supposed to sit quietly so the pairs of officials—one reading aloud, the other tallying—can concentrate. Once in a while our noise level rises and we get shushed like a classroom of unruly children. "Shusssss," a command from the moderator, overseeing the count. Gloria says too loud, "I hate to be shushed."

Darcy says: "Quiet or you'll get gaveled."

Gloria says, even louder: "I hate getting gaveled."

Amos Clark leans toward me, his chair tipping, his big feet anchored to the floor. He says, very serious: "Sorry about your dog."

Gloria stops her defiant whispering. Gloria and Darcy are pretending not to listen to my exchange with Amos Clark. They look the other way, but their silence betrays them.

"My dog is missing," I say. "Have you seen him?"

Amos looks puzzled. "I'm talking about the little dog I thumped with the pick-up. The little brown-and-white dog."

"My dog?"

"Your husband said forget it, but I wanted to say something, you know, the dog run right out. Couldn't get around him."

Amos's wife nods sympathetically, mimes the words "Too bad," as Amos says them.

"I think I'll have some coffee," I say, caffeine shakes already in progress. "Does anybody want some?"

I put my quarter in the can. The coffee dribbles into the Styrofoam cup. I hate coffee and, though I'm politically op- posed to Styrofoam, tonight I've enjoyed the feel of it warm in my hands.

Gloria has followed me to the coffee counter. "What's wrong?" she says. "What was he talking about?"

I picture Buster, flattened. "Christ," I say. "That rat knew all along."

"Amos Clark?"

"Him, too. But Brian, apparently, saw the dog get hit, wrapped him in a blanket, buried him in the corn field and never said a word about it. Meanwhile I'm thinking the dog will turn up any day. I wake up in the middle of the night be- cause I think he's barking outside or scratching at the back door. Sometimes I feel his snuffle on the back of my leg."

"Must have been a ghost snuffle," she says.

Darcy pokes between us. "Brian probably thod he was doing you a favor. That's the kind of thig husbands do." She wipes her nose with a Kleenex ball. "Med cad be so aggravading."

"I'm going to bury *him* in the corn field," I say. "He didn't even show up to vote. If I lose by one vote, I'm going to kill him and bury him beside the dog."

"I would," Gloria says.

·   ·   ·

"ATTEND THE STATUS OF THE VOTE." This from the moderator who's about to have his big moment. The votes have been counted, the results are about to be revealed. My heart pounds with caffeine and dread. Gloria, Darcy, and I levitate to our seats. Since the candidates for selectman are at the bottom of the ballot, those results will be read last. I brace for the wait, remind myself to breathe. Gloria whispers, "I think you've done it. Look at their faces."

I can read nothing in the faces of the Checkers of the Checklist, except a certain smugness at knowing what others do not.

"They're not happy," Gloria whispers. "If Franklin had won, they'd be happy. Look at them. These are people who worship the status quo."

"I thig so too," Darcy says.

I study the Checkers. But to me their faces seem neither happy nor unhappy, simply closed.

Franklin and his entourage have landed behind us—three empty rows back. I turn for a glimpse. Arms folded, legs crossed, they make terse comments to one another from the corners of their proud Pilsnor/Kingsbury mouths. Franklin's voice is so low and manly, his whisper carries across the hall.

He says if he can't beat a non-native like me, he'll move out of town. Franklin Pilsnor's departure (if he stands by his word, which he won't) would be my gift to the community.

I feel hands on my shoulders. They are Brian's hands. He says, "I figured they'd be done by ten. Good thing I came a little early." He's standing behind me wearing the gray wool sweater I knit him three winters ago. The wool over his big, soft belly is warm and a little itchy against the back of my head.

Then I remember how angry I am, and what a rat he has turned out to be. "Why didn't you tell me the dog was dead?"

His hands tighten.

"I thought you had enough to contend with." He sighs. "You were upset enough about Susan."

"Susan!"

"And this damn election."

The moderator, poised for revelation, indulges in a last-minute conference with the Head Checker.

I tip my head to ease the ache in my neck. I study the ceiling. A sturdy metal rod, whitewashed like the plaster, runs east to west, just above the whir of the fans, just above the dangling globes of the fluorescent lights. This slightly bent, rust-scabbed rod looks to be holding the walls upright, as though they have been pushed out of square, tipped outward from the slow, silent explosion of long political controversy. Either that, or the foundation's sinking.

"I should have told you about the dog," Brian says.

I wish Susan were here with us in this town hall among all these strangers. I wish it were our family all together tonight.

Gloria and Darcy lean forward with anticipation, their faces pink and stiff. They are forgetting to breathe. I breathe deep and lean back into Brian's stomach which molds around my ears.

If I win, Gloria and Darcy will leap to their feet and embrace me and embrace each other and we will all hoot with joy. This will embarrass Brian.

If I lose, Gloria and Darcy will deflate like slashed rubber dolls. They will deflate and sink to the floor and I may join them. This will also embarrass Brian.

I wonder how I should react to Franklin Pilsnor when it's over. Should I shake his hand? Should I spit at his proud, smug face? Should I explain, "When I mentioned small potatoes, I wasn't referring to your manly parts but to your rather lax attitude toward certain items in the town budget." Or should I just maintain the quiet dignity of which I know I'm capable.

The moderator reads slowly, repeating each result: first the school district offices, then recreation commission, trustee of trust funds, tax collector. Then: "Office of Selectman, three-year term, vote for one . . ."

God help me, I want to win this election. I want to show Franklin Pilsnor that he is beatable. I want to justify the faith of my supporters. I want to show Brian and Susan and myself just what I can do.

Brian said, "If you win you lose; if you lose you lose."

But he is wrong.

All along, I've said I was running for the good of the town. But the truth is, I needed to run. The truth is, I need to win. I do not know why, exactly, but it has nothing to do with Franklin Pilsnor or his mother-in-law or the strange, incestuous politics of this eccentric little town. And it has everything to do with me.

Brian, the rat, stands solid behind me, as he has all the long years of our marriage. Gloria is squeezing my knee, hard. Darcy sneezes. United, we await the verdict.

The truth is *not* that I lose either way. The truth is, I have already won.

.   .   .

Later, when Franklin Pilsnor drops his impressive set of town-hall keys painfully into my lap, he can't resist a nasty remark. He can't resist what he thinks will be the last word: "You are too stupid to know what you've done," he says, "but you'll figure it out eventually."

An eavesdropping Gooch rushes to my defense, bristling: "Are you addressing your comment to the new selectman?"

I raise my hand to quiet the Gooch. I can handle this. But how? Do I spit? Do I explain? Do I explode? Or do I maintain the quiet dignity of which I know I am capable?

I wait. Franklin Pilsnor steps away, makes for the door, but I stop him with two words. "Small potatoes," I say.

Now he is angry. Now he turns on me, looming. Now his face is red and his toupee quivers.

I smile.

"Small potatoes," repeats the Gooch. "Small Potatoes Pilsnor," reverently, like a witness at a christening.

⚏ The Widow and the Trapper

She called me on the phone. "Come up and trap the beavers," she said.

I'd sooner trap you, lady, I thought.

Then I pictured it: the widow with a tree-set coni-bear sprung on her neck, tongue hanging white as a parsnip.

But I said in a nice way: "Jesus H. Christ, a beaver pelt is worth nothing this time of year."

"But my garden's flooded!"

"I asked you for a permit last winter," I said. "And you said no."

"But the water's nearly up to my back steps," she whined.

The widow lives a mile up the road around the back side of the pond. I can't see her place from mine because of the way the shore curves, but three years ago she parked her trailer on the lowland between the pond and the backwater; now she wonders why her garden's a foot under and the waves are lapping her back steps.

Why she thought I'd trap worthless beaver just to please her, I don't know. But the real puzzle is why the beaver left her alone so long—though they have their cycles like anything else: move into the meadow for a year or two, move out, move on, five years later they're back and you can't drive them away.

I told her to call the warden. "Get hold of Lew Hubbard," I said. "He'll pull the dam and shoot the beaver—or get somebody to shoot them for you."

What did Hubbard do but turn around and call me. "Ray," he said, "I need a favor."

"I know," I said right back, "you want me to shoot the beaver on the meadow."

"Well," he said, "I pulled the dam today. But they'll build it back soon enough. Her trailer's about to float."

It's hard to refuse a warden because, if he chooses, a warden can make a man's life miserable. He can check your traps and ask around about permits. He can make you show your hunting license even though you're old enough for a free one. He can take his sweet time tagging your pelts. He can even count your goddamn fish.

When a warden asks a favor, I try to accommodate.

So I shot the beaver. And I guess the shooting got her attention, because when I arrived back at my truck there she was with her pointy-headed black dog which peeled back its lips and showed its teeth.

"No, no," she told the dog. "Don't you growl at Raymond."

"I think your beaver problem is solved," I told her.

"Do you really?" She tipped up the bill of her Blue-Seal-Feeds cap, hit me in the face with a look from eyes green like fish scales, and smiled her sweet vacant smile. "Well isn't that wonderful!"

I opened the door to my truck cab. The dog jumped in.

"GET OUT OF THERE," I said. The dog lay flat on the seat, growled low like he meant it. I wouldn't have grabbed that dog for a hundred dollars, but the widow reached right in. Small, quick woman with big hands—good for gardening, pull a lot of weeds with those monsters, dig potatoes without a hoe. The dog's neck looked skinny in those hands. "Come on, Puck. You can't go home with Raymond."

I clamped the Stevens into the gun rack, settled behind the

wheel, slid the key in the ignition. "I really appreciate this, Raymond," she said. "Since Mr. Hubbard removed the dam, the water's gone right down. But I do feel bad about the beaver." She pulled a sad face—aged ten years in the process. From under the cap, the gray hair fanned out over each ear like squirrel tails.

I thought: Lady, if you'd stayed in town where you belong, those beaver would be alive today—they could flood that meadow without bothering a soul. Beaver have always lived on the meadow, lady; you're the one who parked your trailer in their way.

I didn't say it at first because the widow can't help the way she is. Then I thought: Why not enlighten her? And I said it.

That was our last encounter for a while—I guess she took offense, which made me think maybe there was more to her than chatter, vacant smiles, and funny hats.

Shortly after the beaver incident the dog got into trouble running deer. Somebody turned him in. She thought it was me, but it wasn't. When I see a dog running deer, I shoot it. Anyway, Lew Hubbard told her she had to keep the dog tied up. I'd anchor my boat in the cove, drop my line in the water, watch the dog run back and forth. Eventually, he ran himself a trench so deep all you could see was his pointy head and flopping ears. Sometimes when I was out in the boat he'd ignore me. Sometimes he'd bark and bark. Sometimes I'd bark back. Usually I'd just peel back my lips and show my teeth.

One morning trolling, I noticed something funny up the cove end, so I headed in that direction. I passed through the shallows, where you have to know your way if you want to keep your propeller out of the sand, steering in the general direction of the widow's trailer—didn't head straight there, making the big swing because trout are more apt to hit on the curve. Eventually, I got close enough to see that some fool had tied plastic float bottles along a rope stretched clear across the cove, from just below the widow's trailer to the point.

"What the hell is going on here?" I said to myself. I cut the engine so I could look the situation over.

Squinting across at her trailer I could just make her out at the window. She knew the story. I had two choices: I could sit in my boat and wonder or I could head over there, find out for sure.

By the time I made up my mind, the widow was down by the water with a pot on her head, motioning me in. She pointed to the landing where the bottle rope was hitched. The dog was, naturally, barking for blood, jumping up and down beside the trench. Every fifth or sixth jump he'd lose his footing and slide in. Pointy-headed dogs are not famous for brains, though they are known to be stubborn. And that's a bad combination in a dog or a human being. When I first met the widow she struck me as particularly brainless—buying that little piece of meadow and parking her trailer there was enough to convince the whole town of that. But she didn't strike me as stubborn until that business of holding a grudge because I questioned her judgment. Then again, I thought, she might not be as stupid or as stubborn as she pretends. Maybe, like everybody else, she's putting on a show. That's the trouble with people—you never really know. With animals, on the other hand, you always know. I've looked into the eyes of a foot-caught coyote and understood it meant to rip my throat out given half a chance—and rightly so.

The widow met me at the landing. The pot turned out to be a pith helmet. "Isn't it wonderful," she said, throwing up her hands.

I climbed out of the boat. The dog's barks were shorter, faster, higher pitched. "How do you stand that noise?" I said.

"Oh, he'll quiet right down," she said. "My alarm system, you know. Gives me fair warning."

I left the boat in the water, tied to a skinny hemlock tree that leaned out from the banking.

"Follow me," she said. "There's a good view not far from here. I've even put a lawn chair out so I can watch in comfort."

She had a pair of binoculars around her neck—the green rubber kind that float.

I let her get fifteen, twenty steps away before following. She didn't even look back to check. "SHUT UP," I said to the dog in passing. He strained to reach me but the cable was strong. He barked high and wild. I grinned my widest grin—see *my* teeth, dog. The dog harked its noise the second we were out of direct line of sight. Guess if he couldn't see us, we must be gone.

The lawn chair sat back from the shore, behind a clump of pussy willow casting whip shadows over the water which rippled when the breeze came. When the breeze stopped, the water cleared and I spotted the pollywogs black and round and still like rotted poplar leaves over the sandy bottom. It's a good clean pond where you can see bottom through six or eight feet of water with the light just right. The sun was behind us. I could feel it on my back.

"You sit," she whispered. When I bent to look where she was looking, the brim of her helmet clunked my skull. "Lean just a little forward, Raymond, and you'll be able to see really well."

"Nothing wrong with my eyesight," I said.

She shushed me, pulled the binoculars off over her head, knocking her helmet in the process. She shushed the helmet.

"The female is there now," she said. "Sometimes she sits; sometimes the male."

I saw the loon and its nest at the east end of what we always called Blueberry Island though it isn't big enough to name: a few bushes, sand, grass, couple rocks. I focused the binoculars on the loon's hard red eye. Still as a wood carving, she knew exactly where we were and what we were up to. The binoculars grew heavy in my hands.

"Does roping off the cove have something to do with loons?" I said. I knew it did, of course, but I wanted her to say so.

"There should be two eggs," she said. "I'm dying to slip over some evening just to check—but they say even a canoe might frighten the adults off long enough for the eggs to cool. So I'm controlling myself."

"Did you put up that rope?" I asked.

"All it would take is one canoe or, God forbid, one motor boat come too close to that little nest. Oh," she said, "I don't know if my heart can stand the strain." She thumped her chest with her big freckled hand. I was thinking how I'd like to thump her helmet down over her eyes and maybe tip her into the drink—just to get her attention. I pictured it: the widow wet and sputtering.

When I got home I called the fish cop. "Hubbard," I said, "there's something funny going on up to the pond."

"What would that be, Ray?" He knew what I meant all right.

"The widow's got a rope across the whole upper end. She's not letting anybody in there."

"I know." From the way he said it, I couldn't tell whether he thought she was in the right or the wrong. Wardens, like any other kind of cop, can talk but say nothing, nod and grunt so you don't know which side they favor. They're not like the rest of us, at least they wouldn't want anybody to think so: We are the law, they say in every way but words, and don't you stinking mushrats ever forget it.

"Explain to me, Hubbard," I said, "how it is that woman can fence off a public body of water like it's a chicken yard."

Hubbard said, "She can block off that loon nest, and she's got every right to do it."

"Who says?"

"The Feds."

I should have known. It's not bad enough they have to mess up my social security every ten minutes, now they're interfering with fishing.

"They've always been loons on the pond," I said. "When I was a kid, a loon laugh just before dark would sit me right up in bed like a sprung jackknife. The only thing worse is a screech owl."

Hubbard laughed—smooth fish-cop laugh.

"I have as much right on that pond as those loons," I said, but I knew there was no point talking to him.

One drizzly morning soon after, she showed up on my doorstep with her head wrapped in cellophane, carrying a cake in a plastic box. Next I knew she was inside, her slicker dripping on my floor. We ate the cake and drank strong coffee. She said: "You haven't brought me any fish yet this season, Raymond. Usually you've brought me fish by now."

"Is that right?" I said.

"Yes," she said. "You've brought me some beautiful trout in the past."

"I haven't been out much," I said. "Afraid I'll forget, catch my propeller in your rope and ruin my motor." Which was true—I hadn't been out much, only because I knew seeing that rope would make me ugly. Instead I'd been concentrating on my woodpile—splitting (each chunk a widow head) and stacking (each half chunk half a widow head) when I should have been fishing. Well, I'd split heads for a few minutes anyway, but splitting wood always calms me right down, helps me think about nothing—my favorite subject.

"Oh, Raymond," she said, "the loons will be hatching soon enough. You'll want to see them."

"Then you'll pull the rope," I said, "after the hatching?"

"You know," she said, "I talked to this woman who lives on Pleasant Lake. They have loons, too. And last summer there were chicks—but this is what happened: a power boat pulling a water-skier chased them down and the next day they were gone."

I thought: Power boats are not your problem, honey. As soon as those things hatch and get brave, they'll be breakfast for some big old snapping turtle. Jaws like bear traps, those snappers. I come across one on the Range Road once—a monster, thirty inches or more across the back. His shell reached almost to my knee. He bit the stick in half, same as he would have done my leg if he could have reached it. I poked, he bit again and would not let go. They don't let go, once those jaws close. . . . If he'd been near home I'd have killed him. Snappers eat more trout than just about anything—except loons. But way up on the Range Road, living in the swamp—I figured what harm was the old bird doing.

But I didn't talk to her about turtles. Instead I said: "When was the last time you saw a water-skier on this pond?"

"There are no water-skiers on this pond. Of course not."

Then I said: "What have you got against fishermen?"

"Nothing," she said. "And if you don't bring me some trout pretty soon, I'll have to become one myself."

"Between the loons and the turtles there won't be any fish left to catch."

"Oh," she said, "I don't believe that for a minute."

When the time for fishing came, she was prepared—I'll give her that. She wore sneakers and overalls, carried a sweatshirt in case the wind picked up. Straw hat tied under the chin kept the sun off. And she had her own pole—useless though it was—a bamboo fly rod belonged to her husband.

I anchored and let her fool with the fly rod for a while. She caught nothing. In this pond, trout hit dry flies only in May and September—but she didn't know that. I gave her what tips I could on placing the fly without hooking herself in the head: "Keep that elbow down—it should touch your ribs. Cast with your wrist smooth and easy. And quit flapping your wings."

I bait fished while she practiced. She caught me just once in the collar and had to needlenose the hook out. If I'd been wearing a T-shirt, she'd have got me right in the jugular, but I said nothing, though all her thrashing gave the fish more warning than they needed about the night crawler on my hook.

"They don't seem to be biting," she said finally. The sun was bright, the breeze died down. The weave of her hat made shadows and sun spots on her face. She seemed discouraged. Though her husband had been a fisherman, she claimed he'd never brought her along. "Fishing was what he did with the boys," she said. "That was his time away, and I never begrudged him."

"Well," I said, "we may be using the wrong ammunition. I've got something here that might bring their appetites back."

I pulled out my fly book, took a golden demon from the felt. "We could troll," I said. "No guarantees, but I've had good luck with this little fella in the past."

She folded the hat brim back with both hands and smiled. Eye to eye with the widow, I saw something there—strong and penetrating as fisher scent (one whiff clears your nose to the middle of your head). I could see she was determined.

I picked up my gallunking pole, looped the leader through the hook eye of the demon, pulled snug. "Just let it out slow," I said.

"The fly is sinking," she said.

"It's supposed to. It's a wet fly."

"I can see that."

"Stop at the end of the yellow line," I said. "Let out all the red, but stop after the yellow. Then the fly will be down where they can get a good look at it."

"Aren't you going to fish?"

"I'll just run the motor awhile," I said, figuring if she did latch on to a good one she'd need help bringing it in. I'd have to net it anyhow. And if she got excited with a second line out, there was apt to be a big tangle. Anything I hate it's separating tangles—which is one reason I fish alone, one reason there's been nobody but me in my boat for a long time—the kind of time that passes without your knowing it because you're thinking of nothing, and content to be.

The widow missed the first strike, and the second. They were biting and would keep on for a while—finicky though, little bit of a temperature change, cloud over the sun, wind shift and they are apt to stop hitting altogether. Sometimes they seem to stop for no reason at all—though I'm sure the reason's there, fish reason.

"You've got to start reeling right away or he'll spit it out," I told her. "Start reeling and just that extra tug ought to be enough to set the hook."

"It startles me when the line moves."

Big soft hands freckled with age spots, she curled one around the grip and placed the other like I showed her with the line under the pad of one finger. "I know we'll catch one soon," she said, leaning forward to try for another eye-to-eye, but I turned my attention quick to my hand on the steering shaft, to the path the motor plowed through the water and the way it curved away behind us.

I thought: Don't you be pulling tricks on me, lady with eyes speckled like tiger trout.

We were on our third pass through the shallows when she began to reel like crazy. She said nothing, just started reeling so hard her knuckles turned white and her face turned red. Well, I thought, now we'll just see, won't we.

After a while, I said: "Can you feel the fish still on?"

"Yes," she said, "he's on. I can feel him pull."

She'd hooked him good. If she didn't do anything foolish, she ought to be able to bring him in.

"Keep your pole low," I said. "Don't give him any slack."

Then I saw the fish leave the water. Silver-blue back in the sun. Big one. She saw it too and gave me a look like she was all-of-a-sudden wide awake. "Keep reeling," I said.

I cut the engine.

From halfway across the pond, I heard the dog barking. The widow was standing in the boat and it seemed like the dog had just then figured out it was her. "Sit down or we'll both be in the drink," I said. It's one thing to stand in an anchored boat, but this one was free-floating and some tippy.

"It won't come anymore," she said. "The reel's stuck. I think it's broken."

"No," I said. "Keep reeling."

I could see her trying, the bones poking out in her wrist. She gave me this what-do-I-do-next look. "Well you don't want to break the line," I said. "That's the last thing you want."

"It's coming, again," she said. "Like it was caught on something and now it's loose. I've lost him."

"No such luck!" I said. "Look at that pole bend. Pull back and you'll feel him."

She reeled some more. I got the net ready, leaned out over the side trying to spot him, then the same complaint: "Stuck again," she said. "I can't move it."

"Betty, there's nothing wrong with that reel," thinking maybe she had lost him. A shame to lose her first fish this close to the boat, and a good big trout too.

But before I could feel too sorry, the real culprit shot out of the water and we could both see what our problem was. The loon wanted the fish. The loon had followed that fish underwater, grabbed it, and stopped progress in mid-reel. He'd let go for some reason, then grabbed it again. Big fish. Sixteen inches at least. A fish like that would make a meal for a man or a woman—or for that big checker-back daddy loon flapping twenty feet off our bow with the fish crossways in its greedy loon beak.

I looked at the loon, then at the woman staring hard into the loon's red eye. She leaned forward—the loon pulled back. She said, "Drop my fish, Loon, or I'll jump from this boat and tear it from your beak with my own hands!"

The loon could see she meant it. He hesitated maybe five seconds—my heart beat three times—then dropped the fish and dived.

She reeled her fish in. "Keep your tip down," I said, "so I can net the foolish thing." Fish measured fifteen and a half inches and weighed just over two pounds.

"What you think of your daddy loon now," I said when she'd finished admiring the fish and congratulating herself.

"I love him," she said. "I think he is magnificent."

"I told you loons eat trout," I said. "Between the four of them, they're apt to eat every trout in this pond."

"Raymond—why do you say such things?"

"That loon almost beat you out of your trout," I said. "It was quite a stand-off for a minute or two, didn't you think?"

"No," she said, using the shirt to wipe the sweat from her face and neck, "you and I both know he never stood a chance."

Then she turned those speckled eyes on me and I saw clear as pond water in afternoon light that she wasn't talking about the loon. And I could see she meant it.

ꟷ Jim's Boat

Jim bought the boat cash with his just-cashed pay check, though he knew Phoebe had the money spent, though he knew she'd pop a gasket when she found out (maybe even because he knew). On his way south with an overload of scrap metal, he spotted the boat for sale in front of a ramshackle estate among the pines—roofed house-trailer, leaning plywood shed, and next to it a school bus with that lived-in look (cement-block steps, curtains, table lamp). He parked his truck on the shoulder and climbed out. Steamy afternoon: black flies pestering but not unbearable, diesel fumes mixing with the tang of hot pine needles. He pulled a handkerchief out of his back pocket and wiped the sweat off his face, fanned himself with his cap, slicked back his hair before snugging the cap back on.

It was an aluminum boat, a seventeen-footer with a deep reinforced hull, not too tippy. He ran his hand along the gunnel. The oars were propped in their locks—ready, it looked like, to propel the boat across the yard. He squatted to check the seams for buckling and the rivets for rust.

Nobody emerged from the house-trailer, though Jim rapped hard on the screen door. The curtains at the small window moved in the weak, hot breeze. Nobody home in the school bus either. The place was deserted except for robins poking for worms, and a dusty cocker spaniel asleep under a dusty lilac bush.

Jim thought: If that boat is still here on the way back, and if there's anybody home to dicker with, why I just might have to make a trade. And he did.

. . .

Before Jim's boat was even off the truck, the kids swarmed it. Phoebe stood in the bulkhead, arms pretzeled across her chest, eyes squinty, head back, neck bony. Only the top half of her showed because she'd climbed just that far up the stairs. They lived in the cellar—that is, the half-buried cement box that would be the cellar when they built the house on top. The floor plan, stained and curled from when the cement sweated, was taped up behind the television, had been taped up there going on four years. The kids knew just where their toy boxes, bureaus and beds were going to sit, even who got the top bunk. Jim wanted a built-in gun cabinet, Phoebe a kitchen full of blond cupboards with matching island. They cut pictures from magazines and pasted them on.

Phoebe's jaw set like Old Man of the Mountain as she watched Jim release the bungee cords that anchored the boat to the truck bed. "Jim," she said, "what is that?"

"It's a boat," Jim said.

"A boat?" she said.

"Kids, tell Ma what this is."

"A boat," the kids said.

She hated when Jim called her Ma. "I'm not your mother," she'd say. "Do I look like your mother?"

Actually, to Jim, she did look like his mother, more so the older she got, especially around the eyes and in the way both their heads tipped, just a little, to one side. Mother tipped right; Phoebe tipped left. He rubbed the head of one glad-to-see-Daddy kid with his open hand—little Ginger hugging his knees. "If you're real good," he said, "maybe I'll take you kids fishing."

An hour later, Phoebe packed up the kids and took off to spend the night at her mother's. Jim put on his bewildered act. "If you don't know, I can't tell you," she said. He slapped the hood of the car as she backed out of the driveway.

After the kids were in bed, she and Lilla ate sliced apple and cheese from an antique china plate and drank Lilla's special iced tea. "He wanted a boat, so he bought one," Lilla said. "That's just Jim. That's just the way he is."

A boat, a snowmobile, a new rifle, a "parts" truck, and God knows what else I haven't found out about yet, Phoebe thought. "We're supposed to be saving for the house, Ma," she said.

"Well, I don't have any money to spare," Lilla said. "If that's what you're hinting at."

Upstairs, the kids slept restlessly. When Ginger rolled into Bunny's back, Bunny hissed: "Stay on your side." And poked her. When Ginger rolled away, the sheet rolled with her. She rolled off the bed onto the floor, but the rug broke her fall. Phoebe found them like that the next morning—Bunny sprawled on the bed in her baby-dolls with no covers; Ginger cocooned in the sheet on the floor. Jim Jr. whined to go home. He wanted to ride his bike. The rabbits needed feeding. His tooth was loose, and Daddy promised to pop it with a string. Maybe Daddy would take them fishing in the new boat. Besides, Phoebe was still stinging from her mother's remark about money. Phoebe would rather live in that cellar hole the rest of her life than take money from Lilla. They went home.

A week later, Jim traded his extra thirty-ought-six and "a couple pesos" for a 15-horse-power Evinrude motor. Lilla said: "Well if he's got a boat, he needs a motor to putt around with, doesn't he?"

"He promised we'd have the house framed this fall. He promised it'd be boxed in by winter," Phoebe said.

"Don't be so hard on him," Lilla said. "You're a hard woman, Phoebe. I don't know where you get it." Phoebe didn't feel hard; she felt soft and easily bruised—like an overripe apple. It hurt to think she might no longer love Jim, though she saw the sweet curve of his mouth and his warm half-moon eyes in the faces of her children.

Of course, she said nothing to him about love or promises. For a month or more, she barely spoke to him, but he didn't seem to notice. On Saturdays and sometimes Sundays through the heat wave, Jim and his boat went fishing with Cousin Willis. They usually took one or two kids with them, which would have meant a break for Phoebe except she had to put up with Willis's fat wife, Glenna, who whined on and on about the high price of coffee, her incontinent dog Russ, her lousy job at the telephone company, the gruesome complications from Willis's vasectomy, and her kids, especially the delinquent, Bobby. Phoebe watched Glenna noodle ice cubes in her diet soda. *God*, Phoebe thought, *at least you don't live in a cellar hole. At least you don't have mold growing on your* Fanny Farmer Cookbook. Phoebe was tired, and Glenna's complaints made her tireder. Meanwhile, the kids that hadn't gone fishing (two of Phoebe's, two of Glenna's) were playing trampoline on Jim Jr.'s bed in the curtained-off corner the kids used for a bedroom. They bounced to the ceiling and screeched like seagulls. Phoebe had tried to forbid the game, but Jim overruled her: "The mattress is no good anyway," he'd said. "They're just having fun. Where's the fun in you, Ma?" He peeked behind her ear. She hit at him, but he caught her wrist, slipped his arm around her back, and twirled her in a way that earlier in their marriage would have made her laugh. "Smile, Ma, smile." He kissed her in the eye. "Pa can make you smile."

. . .

Come fall, Jim and Willis planned to use Jim's boat to tong for oysters down to Great Bay: sea breeze, gulls swooping, the thunk of waves against the hull. Scoop oysters by the basketful, Willis said. All you can eat—raw down the hatch. "They're just laying around in the muck off Nanny Island," Willis said. "But you got to be careful out there—that's the big pond, you know; next stop France."

"Parley voo Frenchy," Jim said.

"Not too good," Willis said.

Jim asked Phoebe did she like to eat shellfish. She said: "What scheme are you thinking up now?"

That hurt his feelings, so he said, "Just wait and see," knowing how wait-and-see made her mad. Sometimes he went out of his way to make her mad. Then he'd stand back while she sparked. He liked to make her spark, so they could make up later—warm and melty.

In the end, it was Glenna who told Phoebe about the planned oystering expeditions. Glenna said: "You priced oysters in the store lately? One trip to the bay and they'll have made back what the licenses cost. I love oyster stew, don't you? And fried oysters. I don't like 'em raw, though. They're gross raw. But they say eating oysters, especially raw ones, is good for you-know-what."

"What?" Phoebe said.

"You-know-what," Glenna said.

That night the kids and Jim crowded together on the couch watching television. Phoebe sat apart from them in the rocker, not watching television. She said: "I will not spend another winter in this cellar without some hope of a house come spring. Do you hear me, Jim?"

"Uh-huh," Jim said. "I know what you mean." The room

was dark except for the television and the fluorescent light in the cubby that served as their kitchen.

"I'm not sure you do," she said. Jim Jr. ran to the television to turn up the sound. A pan of milk was heating on the gas stove. It spilled over and hissed. Jim jumped to grab the pan. Phoebe jumped, too. Jim set the pan on a hot pad, then spooned cocoa powder into mugs lined up on the ironing board. "Did you want some?" he said.

She said nothing. Just stood there staring at the brown, bubbly splotch of milk on the stove.

"Guess not," he said.

He scooped the skin off, poured. He stirred in vanilla and salt, then leaned weakly, mug in hand, against the good-as-new Hot Point refrigerator he'd bought off Joe-the-Appliance-Man for fifty bucks. "If we had the money for the lumber . . ." he said. "Gotta buy studs and spikes, two-by-fours, and all that. For starters. And the time," he said, "where am I going to find the time?"

She locked him out of the bedroom that night with a flimsy hook-and-eye catch he could easily have snapped, but didn't. The kids lined up to watch him tap-tap on the door. Ginger and Jim Jr. looked worried. Bunny looked mad—hair flopped over one eye, chin pushed out, hands in little fists. *One day,* Jim thought, *Bunny will give some man who loves her as much trouble as her mother gives me.*

He cosied up to the door, said Phoebe's name into the crack. The kids stared. "Go to bed," he said, "all of you. Now!"

.   .   .

Phoebe dumped the kids at her mother's. She didn't ask permission. She didn't explain why. She didn't say for how long. She backed up to the garage, loaded her father's chainsaw in

the trunk, then unloaded the kids—shooing them up the walk
and onto the porch. She was back in the car, in third gear and
a quarter mile down the road before her mother, engrossed in
the soaps, got to the door.

At the hardware store, Phoebe bought a quart of chainsaw
oil. In the parking lot, she mixed it with the old gas in the big
red can. She asked Ronny if he'd leave the register a minute,
since there were no other customers, to start the chainsaw for
her. It hadn't been run since her father died—might need a
plug—and if it did, she wanted to know that now. He sold
her a plastic funnel so they could pour from the can to the
tank. And the saw did need a plug. After that, Ronny got it
going on the third pull. He held the saw out from his body
and engaged the chain for a few roaring rotations, to make
sure it was tight.

"Show me how to start it again," she shouted. "Shut it off
and let me start it myself. I don't want it to conk out on me."

"What is it you're sawing up, Phoebe?" Ronny said. "What's
the big hurry?"

She looked at him ugly. "Studs," she said.

.   .   .

Away out in the middle of what had once been Jim's grandfather's hay field stood a large elm tree. The leaves were prema-
turely yellow; the top branches bleached to dry-ki. Phoebe
chose this tree because it was dying, because it stood alone on
top of a small rise, and because it leaned, so the direction of its
fall was predictable.

At the edge of the field, she lifted Jim's boat, one end at a
time, from the sawhorses. Once the boat was on the ground,
she flipped it into float position and launched it on the grass.
With a short rope, she dragged it to within twenty feet of the

dying elm. Then she rested, her long legs stretched out pale, her dress hiked above her knees. She had to put on a dress this morning because she could no longer button her jeans. But it was just an around-the-house dress—no great loss if it got dirty or torn.

There sat Jim's boat, adrift in the grass. Sturdy, dependable, it took him out on the water where he wanted to be, and kept him safe there. She studied the canal the boat had carved in the grass as she'd pulled it through. Some of the flattened grasses and wildflowers were already springing back up. She studied, in the distance, the cement box she'd lived in for four years—flat gray walls, flat black roof, one leggy fuchsia in a hanging basket breaking symmetry. The aluminum arms of the television antenna gridded the sky. The blue hurt her eyes, so she closed them and listened to the bees. She wasn't used to such quiet. So quiet here with no kids around. Peaceful. Warm in the sun. She imagined what it must have been like in the days when Jim's grandfather harvested the hay for his Jersey cows. The swish of air through the grass was like the swish of a scythe. She listened to the hum of traffic on the highway beyond the hill.

She had a plan. She would notch the tree about two feet from the ground to weaken that side and direct the fall. Then she would cut in from behind, wedges handy, just in case. The saw was sharp and would not bind; unlike Jim, her father always kept his saws filed and in working order. She would hold the saw level and steady, letting the chain find its own way in. Once the tree was down and the world stopped shaking, once the boat was flat—flat as a soda can squashed by a Studebaker—everything would be different. Since she couldn't go on with things the way they were, things needed to be different. *Jim will understand*, she thought. *No he won't*, she thought.

. . .

Jim arrived home that afternoon, kidneys sore from the bouncing of the truck; jockeys wedged from the long, hot sit; shirt soaked and sticky and too tight through the shoulders. He was worn down, seeking relief in several forms: a welcome from his wife, a shower, a cold drink, a good meal, a romp with the kids, then an hour or two on the pond bait fishing in the cool of evening with Willis and a cold six-pack.

Phoebe had done a washing. Good sign. There hung five pairs of his jeans side by side on the clothesline, the waists pinned to the rope, the legs stiff and dark—like the jeans of five invisible levitating men. He climbed out of the truck, half expecting to be tackled by a rowdy kid or two; half expecting an ambush; half expecting them to rush out, trip him up; half expecting the clamp of small arms around his legs, or his breath knocked out by a little head cannonballed into his groin. But no kids appeared. No Phoebe either. All quiet on the home front.

Too quiet.

He headed for the door, but before he reached the bulkhead something strange and bright out in the green field caught his eye, something out of place a way out beyond the levitating men. "What the . . ." he said, squinting. His eyes were sore from the long ride, sore and blurry from driving into the sun.

The sawhorses behind the shed stood empty. That was his boat sitting in the field. Just sitting there. And Phoebe on the center bench, just sitting there, staring at the big elm tree.

"Phoebe," he shouted. "What the heck?" He felt like laughing, she looked so funny sitting in a boat in the middle of a hay field. He ran in her direction, fast at first, then slowing to catch his breath, then skipping and acting like he wasn't in much of a hurry. "What the heck?" he said when he saw the chainsaw at the foot of the tree, the little pile of sawdust, the notch in the trunk.

He walked up to the boat, put his hands on the gunnel and rocked it a little to get her attention. She looked at him. Her eyes were wide and blank. Her hands were curled under the plank seat as though she were bracing herself for a wild ride. He climbed in beside her. "Where are my kids?" he said. "There seems to be a few kids missing."

"Not here," she said, then she leaned her head into his shoulder, all tired out. "The kids are at my mother's."

"It's Tuesday," he said. "What they doing over there on a Tuesday? Ain't Tuesday her bowling day?"

"I was going to cut the tree down," she said. "I thought it might make good lumber. Glenna said it's got Dutch elm disease. She said it's dying. But it's not dead yet."

"Elm's no good for lumber," he said. "What were you gonna do, haul the wood back in the boat? Probably a wheelbarrow woulda worked better, don't you think?"

She unclenched her fingers from the plank seat, took his hand and spread his fingers wide over her stomach. The cotton of her dress was soft and loose, damp from her sweat and his. They sat a long time together, just that way, her head tipped into his shoulder, his fingers studying the curve of her belly. Jim's boat floated silver in the grass, the asters purple-blue, the goldenrod waving, the waves swelling ominously.

⚓ Fishing with George

My dad's buddies call him Cub and so do I. Some people call him Mal; my mother calls him Malcolm when she's mad at him which she is today.

Cub calls everybody George including me. Unless it's an emergency like I'm about to step on a slippery rock and the current's too strong. Then he'll shout, "Jeannie Farr, watch your step." Just about the only time my dad gets mad is when he's scared like that or when my mother drives him to it—which she did last night, which is why we are out fishing for the day; so everybody will cool off and remember they love each other.

We don't talk about love in our family. But we feel it. I do. I love my dad and mom and even my little brother whose real name happens to be George. Cub calls him little George to distinguish him from all the big ones.

Cub, George, and I are fishing for pickerel on the bog end of Macon Pond. Cub's friend Colby Fifield has come along too. He is a bearded man with small black eyes which I call shifty because they look to the right and left but never straight ahead. Mom says he treats his women like dogs and his dogs badly. But Cub likes him a lot.

From the back of the boat where he's running the motor, Colby says, "What-ya-think? Mouth of the brook, Cub?"

"Anywhere along there, George," Cub says. "Muck is muck; weeds is weeds." My dad is easy-going. Everybody likes him.

Everybody likes my mom too. Her smile is a beam of light. She shines it on people and they can't help smiling back. I believe they are the two most likable parents in the world. The puzzler is how come they get along with everybody else but not with each other.

Colby spits into the water, then pulls the steer bar sharply so the boat thumps its own wake with a high-flying spray. Today we're in Cub's flat-bottom boat he calls "The Pickerel" because it's for pickerel fishing and also it's dark green like a pickerel. Cub's motor broke, so we're using Colby's, so, naturally, he has the privilege of running it. Colby's a big man, the boat rides low at his end, and when the wake hits he gets splashed good. So do George and I in the bow. The water is cool and surprising. Cub, in the middle seat, grins when the spray touches him.

George pinches me because my leg accidentally touched his. For punishment, I grab him by the shoulders; he squirms but can't fight hard because if he rocks the boat there'll be trouble. I give him a wet kiss on the side of the head where his crewcut is peach fuzz. "Jesus," he says just loud enough for me to hear over the putt-putt of the motor.

"What's that, Little George?" Cub says. "Did you make a comment?"

"Can I row?" George asks.

"Don't need to row. George's motor is running beautiful."

"I mean when we get in the weeds, can I? When we get fishing?"

Since George rows in circles, I'm pretty sure Cub won't let him. Cub says, "I'll think about it." Which means no. I'm glad.

This morning Mom didn't get up with us for breakfast. Last night she made supper, but wouldn't eat any of it. Also, she made liver, onions, and lima beans which we hate. She's mad because of Cub's new gun. He collects them. Sometimes on payday he brings home a new one. Sometimes this makes her mad. This time it made her really mad.

George hid in the clothes hamper. I stayed put on the couch, pulled the afghan over my head and tried to hear T.V. instead of them in the kitchen where the liver was frying loudly.

Mom scolded. Cub said Yup-Yup-Yup like he was agreeing with her. Then he took the gun through to the cabinet in their bedroom. I glimpsed it as he passed between me and the television: oily-black barrel, golden stock with a rubber shoulder rest, dark leather sling. It was a big gun, long and heavy. He carried it tight to his chest, the barrel against his cheek.

Back in the kitchen, he tried again. But she wouldn't laugh, let him change the subject, or swill a nice cold drink to calm her nerves.

She slammed supper on the table. Browned onions flew. I asked if George and I could eat in front of the T.V. "No!" she said. So we had to sit there watching Cub eat. Watching her not eat. I concentrated on rolling lima beans into my sleeve to flush later. After a while, she said to Cub: "Does the word responsibility mean anything to you?"

He ignored her and drank coffee with his nose in the cup.

After a while she said: "Do you ever think?"

"Sometimes," he said.

Then she said, "Do you ever think one day ahead? Do you ever wonder what this family will do for money a week from Thursday? Do you, Malcolm Farr? Do you?"

She kept after him: Do you this, Malcolm Farr? Do you that? Then, when everybody was real quiet, George spilled the milk.

That did it! Milk sloshed in the liver platter, bread flew when Cub tried to knock it clear, the pepper tipped end over end, a white pond spread over the oilcloth downhill toward

George who pushed his chair back too fast and fell off. There was yelling and crying. Mom tried to mop the milk up with a rag but it drizzled off the table onto George anyhow. Cub bent to pick George up. The rag dripped milk on Cub's head. He said, "Watch it!" My mother didn't like his tone, so she threw the rag full force and didn't miss. Then Cub got mad.

He turned white, his eyes fired up, and the hair in his eyebrows stood out stiff. He said: "You kids get to your room NOW." We ran for it, but I wasn't fast enough so he gave me a little shove to help me along, but I was already headed so I toppled into the washing machine. My pink butterfly glasses flew, hit the wall, and broke in half at the nose.

Today they're taped together and cross-braced with a straightened-out paper clip. Cub says I can get some new ones next payday. He says it's about time I had new glasses—which I believe because a few days ago at dusk I looked out across the yard at a sawhorse and thought it was a cow.

.   .   .

I lean over the side of Pickerel to try to grab a white lily with a pink center. Cub says: "Don't tip the boat, you Georges." George fishes with rubber worms. He waves one in my face, but it doesn't bother me so long as I don't get hooked in the eye. His first cast lands on a rock sticking out of the water. I laugh. He glares and starts to reel in. I say, "Nice shot, George."

My dare-devil sails through the air and splats down just where I aim it. It's a big lure because I'm interested in big fish, the kind Cub can filet out from the main bones, the small bones sliced criss-cross so they don't stick in your throat.

Bringing home some tasty pickerel might cheer Mom out of her mad fit since she loves them fried—not as much as smelts but almost. A fish feast might just straighten things out.

I'm pretty sure things are going to straighten out eventually because they've had big fights before and always made up. But I'm not positive. I'm old enough to know that hoping doesn't make it so. Like Grampa Mac got sick, went to the hospital, took a turn for the worse, and that was the end of him. Like Uncle Jay and Aunt Lana seemed to be getting along fine but the next thing you know the house is sold, Jay moves to Vermont, and Lana makes herself sick not eating because she thinks she's too fat which she isn't fat at all.

Cub made his lure himself—a small carved fish, bluish with red spots and a lead belly-fin. He likes to try different things—a spoon, a fly, live bait, a spinner. Same when we go blueberrying. Mom, George, and I find a good bush and pick it clean. Cub goes off looking for a better bush. Sometimes he walks the whole power line looking for a better bush and hardly picks anything at all.

"Ain't you fishing, George?" Cub says to Colby.

"I'm waiting until the time is right," Colby says.

"What will you do to pass the time until it's right?"

Colby leans forward and pulls a beer from the cooler at his feet. "I'm going to drink some beer," he says.

Cub says, "No sense putting it off."

I'm glad Cub has a friend like Colby to do things with when it gets bad at home. But I'm a little afraid of him sometimes. I don't know why—maybe his loud voice or shifty eyes or the way his spit glands work overtime. To me, Colby Fifield always seems mad, even when he's pretending not to be. He makes me twitchy; he makes my stomach tight—which feels like being afraid. George thinks I'm afraid of nothing. But I'm afraid when Mom and Cub fight: I'm afraid there's a hole in our family that gets bigger every time.

"I want to fish with bellies," George says, because Colby caught a big one on the belly of a small one.

Pretty soon we're all fishing with bellies. Colby drinks the last beer. Then he stands and pees over the side. George and I pretend not to notice. There's fish blood on the bottom of the boat which rocks when Colby sits back down.

.   .   .

The beer is gone and the apples are gone and we're all hungry for lunch. George has been complaining for an hour and he's not lying: his stomach growls so loud mine growls back.

We head home across open water, loaded down with picker-el—the bellies did the trick. Colby pushes the motor wide open and we skim. I like the wind in my eyes and the way my hair blows all over my face. The wind dries the fish slime and pond water on my hands, arms, sweatshirt, jeans.

We're just off the landing when Colby shuts the motor down and nods for Cub to row us in. Colby's fiddling with the big butterfly nuts that clamp the motor to the back of the boat. One is stuck, so he kneels on the seat for leverage. Cub can't row with Colby's big rear end in the way so we sit and watch the struggle; he can't seem to get a grip.

"Do you suppose it's stripped, George?"

Colby growls.

"I got some WD-40 in the truck. Wait'll we get to shore and we'll give it a squirt."

"Don't need it," Colby says. "I'll just give her a good yank."

He stands. The boat rocks, rights itself. I take a deep breath: this water is too cold for swimming; also it's hard to swim with a boat on your head. I grab George's hand and hold tight.

"Watch it, George!" Cub yells.

Colby yanks straight up on the motor, and then a bad thing happens.

Instead of the motor pulling off the wood, the top planking

kind of dissolves—rotten I guess—and there's this gap in the back of the boat which startles Colby so he loses his balance and lets go. The motor, still attached to a ragged section of wood, sinks into the dark water of Macon Pond.

I'm afraid we're going to sink. George and I are sitting on flotation cushions; my plan is to hold on to my brother and those cushions for dear life.

Cub says to Colby, "George, you broke my boat."

Water pours through the gap. Colby just stands there, staring at the place in the water where his motor went down.

We hear a shriek from shore. It's Mom. She's probably brought lunch—which I didn't think she would because of the fight. She's hopping beside the car at the water's edge. She shouts: "Malcolm, bring those kids in this minute. You're sinking!"

Cub says, surprised: "We may sink. It's a possibility," too soft for her to hear, which is just as well.

Colby stands and stares. We stop sinking the second he jumps overboard. Like his motor, he's there at the back of the boat one minute and gone the next, feet first into the water. The splash is spectacular.

Free of his weight, the back end pops up and the leaking stops.

Mom shouts, "Oh my God! Malcolm be careful."

I can tell by the way she says his name that it's not just us kids she's worried about. I wave to her. I poke George. He waves too. She beams at us, weakly, like her batteries are low. I try to beam back. This is something I've been practicing for a while.

Cub calls down into the water, "Where are you, George?"

No answer. No nothing.

Then we notice a commotion. Between the boat and the landing, something is moving just under the surface. Not swimming, but moving in the general direction of shore. I think of hippos on *Wild Kingdom* lurking in the muddy waters of the Nile. Then we see what might be a muskrat but turns out to be the top of a man's head. Then we see his neck and shoulders. Then his broad, soaked back.

Colby Fifield is walking out of Macon Pond with his motor in his arms. I can see it clearly now. The white propellers, the greasy shaft. He holds it out from his chest and walks not-too-steady, but making headway. The water weights his legs and almost trips him, but he pushes forward and through. Water to his waist, to his knees, ankle deep, green pond weed dragging behind, and he's out. Water streams down his back and legs; his boots squish loudly. He nods to Mom, walks around the Chevy and up the hill. He drops the motor into the back of Cub's truck.

Cub says, "We better head in before your mother gets herself all worked up." She looks worked up—arms folded across her chest, back straight as a rod, hair falling in her face. She unfolds her arms just long enough to push her glasses into place on her nose. She has the kind of nose glasses always slide down—especially when she sweats.

George says, "Can I row?"

Cub says, "No."

"She's still mad," I say, low. Colby is sitting in the truck cab with the windows rolled up. Cub says, "She's mad all right." He takes up the oars with a flourish—my fine, strong, slightly drunk father. He raises his voice so she'll be sure to hear: "When I married this woman," he says REAL LOUD, "I knew she was quick to lose her temper. And I knew she stayed mad a long time. It's part of her charm—God love her!"

My mother raises her fist and shakes it in our direction. "You're drunk or you wouldn't dare say such a thing to me. I don't know why I put up with you, Malcolm Farr. But it could be worse—I could be married to *him*." She points with her finger and arm and whole body at Colby Fifield, a dark wet lump in the truck. Colby rolls down the window, sticks his arm out, gives her the bird.

"I'm not drunk," Cub says. "Though I have had something to drink. Don't hurt him, George," he says. "George is having a bad day."

"Don't George me, Malcolm Farr," she says. "Don't you *ever* George me."

Well, I think, Cub and Mom are speaking to one another. This is a good sign. The boat didn't sink. This is another good sign. We head for shore with the steady dip and dip of our oars into the black water of Macon Pond. "Look ahead for that big rock, Jeannie Farr," Cub says. "We don't want to hit it at this late date and sink ourselves."

"I'm watching," I say. George and I are both craning our necks, looking sharp as we can for the ledge we know lies just under the surface, just off-shore. We know where it is, in the shadow of the peeling birch, but sometimes it moves a little—a few feet one way or the other—to keep us alert. My mother steps closer to the water, another inch and she'll be wading. She's in position to catch the rope and pull us up on shore.

"Be right there, George," Cub says to Mom. "Any sign of that ledge, Georges?" he says to my brother and me.

"I'm watching," I say. "Don't see anything yet, but I'm watching. My eyeballs are peeled."

✦ Three

The cat has been in the tree now for seven days, we think. Anyway, she's been missing seven days and that first thunderstormy night we looked all over for her and the next day, too. I was broken up about it, imagining her wet and cold and lost. After a week, we figured she was dead—flattened in the road or eaten up by a fisher cat. Nobody thought to look in the big tree until this morning when I was out early picking dandelion greens. Mum said one more day and the greens would be bitter, so I was not to come back until the bag was full. For a joke, Daddy said let them blossom and we'd nip a thousand heads for dandelion wine.

He grew up on a farm. His father made dandelion wine. Daddy loved farms and hated when we lived on Main Street, Soucook. But sometimes bad luck is good luck. We had to move out of the apartment when Daddy got hurt, because he couldn't climb the stairs or work anymore at the mill. But we get to live on the farm passed down from Aunt Lena Boudreau who lived to be ninety-nine but wasn't much on upkeep. And our field is full of dandelions. And we might even get a goat or a cow or chickens.

While picking greens I pictured how scared the cat must have been during the storm, how scared I would have been out in that cold, hard rain with lightning touching down and thunder pounding the world. I was scared in my new room with the window shut tight. Since we moved to the farm, I don't sleep with my little brother, Warren, anymore, and it was lonely when the lightning flashed so bright I could see it through my closed eyelids. On such a wild night the cat would surely have come home if she could. Our old man neighbor, whose one ear is so much bigger than the other his cap tilts, says cats are fishers' favorite snack. He says cats don't last long in fisher country.

The cat must be dead, I thought as I rested on the prickly grass, my bag not half full of dandelion greens, and I thought about the neighbor, the oldy-moldy smell of him and the way his silver whiskers poked out through his skin like a thousand tiny needles. *Dead, not suffering*. Then I heard this funny sound over my head.

I froze. Was it a fisher about to pounce?

But no, it was the cat mewling from a half-way-up branch in the big pine tree by the stone wall. She didn't look good: skinny, wet, bedraggled. Her head was small. Her eyes were big. She called to me. She said: I've been up in this tree seven days and I'd like to get down now.

Poor cat has not been the same since we moved out of our apartment on Main Street, Soucook, along the bonny bonny banks of the Soucook River. Daddy calls them the bonny bonny banks after a song, but they're just clay, rocks, cans, and car parts. My name is Bonny, so when he sings bonny bonny banks, the joke's on me.

When we cleared our stuff out of the apartment, the cat was the last to go. Warren and I found her behind the toilet making herself small. She hissed and tried to snag me when I reached for her. We both missed. Mum brought a cardboard box with flaps. "Kittywinks," she said, "you'll be happier on the farm. You'll have all outdoors and there won't be many cars so you won't have to worry about being flattened."

On Main Street, Soucook, cats who roamed the streets

didn't last long, which is why we kept ours always inside except
when Warren took her out on the fire escape to touch new
snow. He stuck her front paws in it. She twisted free, then hun-
kered down beside the garbage barrel. After that, she was terri-
fied of any open door.

When Warren scooched down to try and grab the cat behind
the toilet, I tugged him back. "The cat is not in a good mood,"
I said. "She'll hurt you."

He elbowed me in the stomach so I'd let go. It didn't hurt;
he's just a little guy. Warren doesn't like to be touched. Especially by me. Sometimes I have to touch him though, to protect
him. He's always into something. If Mum and Daddy and I
didn't keep our eyes on him, he'd be dead by now—drowned
probably in the Soucook River. He loves the river. When we
lived in the apartment, he headed for it every time we let him
out of our sight. Out the door, down the stairs, across the parking lot, over the fence, through the weeds, heading for the
water. Usually he didn't make it past the fence, because it
is a tall one and he's just a little guy. The time it took him to
scramble the fence, somebody'd catch up with him. Once,
though, he made it to the footpath along the bank. Once he
made it to a flat rock six feet offshore. Luckily the river was
low. Luckily he didn't lose his balance because even in a
foot of water, Daddy says, the current is strong enough to
knock a little guy over and pull him in.

I used to love the river too. I used to love how the water
moved between the banks, over and around the rocks. I
watched the water pictures changing moment to moment,
moving pictures brown or blue or gray or black, or a combination swirled together depending on the light.

Sometimes when the water was high and the sky overcast,
the rocks seemed like knuckles and the water a smooth brown

glove. I imagined I could walk across the river, knuckle to knuckle.

My best friend, Marylou Randlett, and her three brothers lived upstairs from us on Main Street, Soucook. Carl, the oldest, is in high school; Joshua and Jeremy (I call them the J's) are both in seventh grade because Joshua stayed back. The boys wear flattops and look alike: dirty blond hair, greeny eyes, dimples deep enough to poke a finger in. Carl is about twice as big as the J's—but they're sprouting up. Joshua has a scar from the corner of his right eye to his ear where Jeremy got him with an arrow playing cowboys and Indians. Everybody says it's a lucky thing he didn't lose his eye. The J's liked to pick on Marylou and me because we were girls and younger and smaller. Mum said they picked on us because they liked us— but she was wrong. They picked on us because they're mean. Marylou and I pretended we didn't care. Pledge number two of the BonnyMalou Club: Ignore the J's when they're gross or mean. Pledge number three: If they hit, hit back harder.

But Carl was nice—and smart, too. He explained to me how a heart pumped blood. He drew ventricles and arteries in the clay of the Soucook River. He clenched his fist to show how big his heart was. I clenched mine too and, when no one was looking, curled it against my chest for fit.

Marylou said I should marry one of her brothers when I grew up, then we'd be sisters-in-law. I told her I'd pick Carl, but don't ever tell him that! "Me, too," she said.

The J's liked to fish the Soucook River. They caught great brown gasping fish with dinosaur fins flaring on their backs. Sometimes they killed the fish by smashing their heads on the rocks. Sometimes they stabbed them with their penknives. Sometimes they cut their organs out and threatened to make Marylou and me eat them. Sometimes they just threw the fish back to catch another day, because fish from the Soucook are not really fit to eat except by cats. The Randletts had lots of cats which ran loose and often got flattened in the road. Still, there was never a shortage, and sometimes the J's brought home fish for a big cat feed.

When we moved to the farm we kept our cat inside for a while just like at the apartment. We didn't want to shock her with too many changes all at once. But Mum said she was never going to buy another bag of kitty litter once this one was used up. No need now that we lived in the country. She said there weren't enough cars on our road to worry about. She put the cat on the screen porch for a couple of days with the outside door propped open a few inches. The next step was to coax the cat out on the grass and hold her. The cat wanted to run back to the house, but Mum held her still. I stroked under the cat's chin and she started to purr. "You see, Kittywinks," Mum said, "it's not so bad out in the world." She tickled the cat with a stalk of grass. She threw a small stone. The cat chased it. Nervously, the cat discovered the world, each day spending a little more time outside, always coming in before dark to sleep on my bed, always at my feet when I woke from bad dreams and needed something to cuddle. Until one night at bedtime, the cat was nowhere to be found. Mum and Daddy and I took flashlights and spiraled the field like fireflies. We pushed into the woods, calling and calling. Calling and listening. We searched the world.

But all we found was Warren, who was supposed to be asleep but had sneaked down the stairs and out across the field in his pajamas and bare feet. The bugs were biting him raw. "Warren!" Mum said, scooping him up. She was crying because of the cat and so was I.

Daddy wrapped his shirt around Warren's bitten feet and

walked home in his undershirt. The mosquitoes raised welts all over his arms and neck. He didn't seem to mind. I know he wished he could be the one to carry Warren. But he can't lift anymore, nor raise his arms over his head since the accident at the mill. Daddy said we should all stop crying because the cat would be back in the morning.

Bad things come in threes, Mum said. When the cat didn't come back the next morning or the next or the next, she said it was number three and thank God for that. Number three meant our run of bad luck was over. First Marylou, then Daddy hurt bad, then the cat. She loves the cat. She loves the cat so much she doesn't even mind when it hurts her. When she pulled the cat from behind the toilet, she got scratched so hard blood ran down her arms. She and I, of all the family, love the cat best.

The day after the cat disappeared I walked to the neighbor's to see whether she might have gone there by mistake. The neighbor gave me a fireball. He keeps a pocketful for all the pretty girls he meets. The fireball burned my mouth, but I ate it anyway so as not to be rude. He was sucking on one too, rolling it around in his mouth like a loose tooth. The fireball made his lips red. He hadn't seen the cat. He smelled like the hundred-year-old grease Mum scraped off the cook stove in the farm kitchen. That's when he told me: "Don't you know fishers love to eat cats? Don't you know pound-per-pound a fisher is the most vicious animal alive?"

We didn't know there were fishers around. Mum would never have put the cat out if she thought there was danger. On the walk home I pictured danger as a fierce-eyed animal crouched in the bushes. I pictured danger as the black tread of a tire bearing down. I pictured danger as the smooth brown glove of the Soucook River closing its fingers over my head.

But seven days later *the cat is alive* in the big pine tree, mewling from a half-way-up branch. "Kittywinks!" I say. "I don't believe it. Come down. Come-ere, kittykittykiddy."

The cat doesn't move. She looks down and wails, but she doesn't know how to get down. Maybe that's why she's been up there seven days.

"Then stay put," I say. "I'll be right back with help."

I leave the bag of greens and run for the house. As I'm running, I'm thinking about luck and miracles. It's as if the cat has come back to life by a miracle. It's as if anything is possible now that the cat is alive.

After the neighbor scared me about the fishers I figured probably the cat was dead. As days passed, I became sure of it. I knew at my heart the cat was dead. And those things I know at my heart have always turned out true.

But no, I'm running for help and reliving the dream in which Marylou smiles because I'm so surprised to see her alive. "Put your eyeballs back in your head, Bonny," she says. "I'm not dead. Jeremy drowned, not me. I'm alive, Bonny."

I feel light as the field grass that scratches my legs as I run. I feel light as the wind I make with my running, wind that lifts my hair off my forehead and cools my face.

"Mum," I call. "Mumma!" She's at the screen door. "The cat." I am breathless from running. "It's in the tree."

She closes her eyes.

"In the big pine tree by the wall."

She says, "Warren, run down to the garden and get your father. Tell him we've gone across the field for the cat."

I tug her down the steps. "Come on," I say. "I'll show you."

She tells me to slow down and holds my hand tight. "I don't want to trip in a woodchuck hole and break something," she says. It takes a long time to cross the field with Mum holding me back. I'm afraid the cat will have disappeared by the time we get there. I'm afraid I imagined the cat in the tree or dreamed it. I'm afraid it's some other cat, not our own but a smaller, darker cat with three white paws instead of four.

We stand at the base of the tree and look up. The cat looks down. "Kittywinks," Mum calls, "kittykittykiddy." The cat looks very small, but she has four white paws. She cries for us. She is high in the tree—higher in the tree than our house is tall—and there are no low branches for us to climb. Mum stretches her arms to the cat, but I can see that nothing in its right mind would jump such a distance.

Mum says, "I thought you were gone for good, Kittywinks. I thought you were the third bad thing."

I understand why Mum isn't so happy to see the cat as I am. If the cat is alive, then the third bad thing hasn't happened yet. If the cat is alive there's bad luck still to come. This makes me sick at heart. I think of Warren who is always into something. I think of matches in the barn, abandoned wells, miles of woods and swamp to get lost in. I've heard about these dangers on the news, about what happens to kids who stray too far or make mistakes. Marylou was on the Channel 9 News. They showed the river bank. They showed the men searching for her body. They showed her all wrapped up and being carried by strangers.

Mum stands on tiptoe and stretches her arms over her head. The loose sleeves of her dress fall back, exposing the white of her arms. Her head is tipped as far as her neck can stretch, exposing her soft under-jaw and the hard curve of her windpipe.

After a while she drops her arms and looks at me with bright eyes: "Bonny, I think we're going to need a ladder," she says.

I am running to tell Daddy about the ladder. I can see him and Warren just starting out across the field. The cat has come back to life: maybe our bad luck has turned good. The cat survives. Daddy's back will heal. I live the dream in which Marylou is saved and Jeremy is the one who died. Marylou is smiling and I am smiling back.

But I know the dream is a bad one. You can't trade the living for the dead. It is wrong to dream such a thing or to wish it. The J's teased her to the edge. They laughed when her foot stuck in the clay. They laughed when she tipped over. They did not push her. They reached for her, but she was used to pulling away and pulled too far. Jeremy tried to save her. He and Joshua nearly drowned themselves trying. Sometimes mean boys are also brave. When she slipped away they jumped in after her.

I tried to call out to her. I watched her sink so slowly she should have been able to catch at the bushes, should have been able to grab the root, or cling to the boulder or touch her brother's hand which was right there, easily within her grasp if only she'd turned and reached for it. I tried to call out so she could catch at my words and pull herself back on them.

When I saw the pictures moving over her I recited our first pledge: Friends forever, never parted. Then I forgave her for breaking it.

Carl was on the hill and saw her slip. He ran toward the river, but the freight train came and cut him off. By the time he reached us, Joshua had all he could do to save himself, and Carl saved Jeremy. But Marylou was gone.

Mum and Daddy and Warren and I *had* to leave our apartment on Main Street, Soucook, because it was too sad for us living downstairs from a dead girl's family, hearing their footsteps on our ceiling, hearing their voices and never hers.

·   ·   ·

The neighbor's extension ladder almost reaches the branch below the branch to which the cat clings. Daddy says, "I'm not so crippled up I can't climb a ladder. My legs still work fine."

Mum says, "No." She means it. Daddy turns his face away and Mum curls her hand over his shoulder. Daddy curls his hand over Warren's head.

Warren says, "I want to climb up. I'm a monkey."

"You're a monkey all right," Daddy says.

The neighbor says, "Something chased that cat up there and scared her so bad she's decided to stay put until the coast is clear. Only thing, she's still too scared; she doesn't realize. If you try to grab her, she'll just climb higher. What you should have, really," he says, "is a safety strap like the lumberjacks use to top off. That ladder could slip pretty easy even with us holding steady. Wouldn't take much of a slip from that height."

He brought the ladder in his pick-up truck. It is aluminum with adjustable feet to grip the pine-needley ground. It touches the tree just below the branch where the cat crouches. Someone at the top of the ladder could easily reach the cat. I hope she will decide to climb down on her own.

The cat makes herself small. She looks like a bird's nest.

Mum says, "I'll climb the tree." She smiles at Daddy. "You always said I was nimble, Paul."

"I'd leave the stupid thing be," the neighbor says. "She'll come down eventually if an owl doesn't get her."

When Marylou died Mum said it could just as easily have been me. She cried all night, rocking me in the big chair like when I was a baby with an earache. I didn't want her to rock me. I didn't want to be touched by her, or by anyone. I wanted to curl up on my bed like a stone. But she wouldn't let me go. She *would not* let me go. So instead, I turned to stone on her lap. I must have slept some because all of a sudden it was morning and weak pink sunlight touched the window while the streetlights still burned.

The neighbor says, "Put some cat food down below and wait a couple days. She'll climb down when she gets hungry enough." He says to me, "How many cat skeletons you seen in trees lately?"

"I don't know," I say.

"Cats go up; cats come down," he says. "They all come down eventually."

I am sure the cat will never come down. I know at my heart she will cling to that limb until she dies unless someone is brave enough to rescue her. But I don't want Mum to be the one, because the third bad thing could be the ladder slipping and her falling—falling and falling with the cat in her arms, the cat digging in, then pushing away, leaping clear to save herself. The cat and Mum like a shooting star split in two, separating in mid-air—both falling the long fall but only one with nine lives. This, too, makes me sick at heart.

I am out of reach before anyone notices. They don't dare follow because two on the ladder is too many. "Bonny, come down," Mum says. "I mean it."

Through the soles of my sneakers I feel the curve of each rung. I step carefully, curling my feet just so to match the curve. It is like walking on the knuckles of a smooth brown glove. Tricky, but I can do it. I am doing it.

They are shouting for me now but I block out the sounds. I do not look down.

I move my right hand up, hold fast. Then my right foot. Then my left hand. I hurry a little. My left foot slides and I gasp. But my right foot and my hands hold firm and I am all right.

I am all right.

I am high and close to the trunk. The smell of pine fills me. I can see the streaks of pitch on bark so deeply pitted I could almost wrap my arms and legs tight around and find a hand-hold and climb the trunk itself.

I do not look down.

I look up. I hear Daddy's voice: "That's far enough, Bonny. Hold tight."

I hear Mum: "Leave the cat. Just come back down. Come down now."

The hardest thing is not obeying my mother.

"Kittykittykiddy," I say. "Come-ere, Kittywinks."

The cat backs away. She is a foot out of reach. I climb one more rung.

Then I hear the thumping and I feel the trunk vibrate. I look down. The neighbor is pounding the trunk with a big rock—to get the cat's attention, I think. Thump, thump, thump. "Here kitty," I say. I throw her a rope of words. "Come to me, kittykittykiddy."

I climb one more rung.

The cat stretches to see where the thumping's coming from and I grab her by the back of the neck. She is too weak to fight. She hangs like a bag of onions. I fold her against my chest with one arm like I do sometimes at night when I need something to cuddle.

I back down a rung. I find I can cling to the ladder with one arm and one foot carefully placed.

I find another rung and another and another. The cat lies quiet. I look down. The arms are reaching for me. I loosen my hold on the cat. She climbs on my neck and digs in. My foot slips, but this time I don't save myself. The cat is on my neck and I am falling away from the ladder. The arms are reaching but the ladder is falling too. The ladder and I hit the ground at the same time. My leg snaps under me. I hear the snap and I feel it all over. I am thankful I didn't land on the ladder or the ladder on me. I am lying in pine needles. My mind is blank with pain.

The neighbor has the cat by the neck. "I'll put this thing in the house," he says. "And call the Rescue Squad. Unless you want to try driving her in the truck?"

"Call Rescue," Mum says. Her hands are all over me. My mother's hands. My father's hands. Warren's little hands.

"I hope to God it's only the leg," Daddy says.

"Bonny, I don't know what got into you," Mum says. "I really don't." She is crying again, just tears, no sound, a quiet river of tears. But this will be the end of it. This will be the end of our crying for a long time because—snap—my leg is broken and that, finally, makes three.

⚓ Marymay's Eyes

I should not have been eavesdropping through the heating grate between the downstairs parlor and the upstairs hall in Gram and Gramp's house, but I was; the cousins dared me. We were mad because we'd been chased out: "Go upstairs and play, all of you!" We wanted to know why the grownups were so grim and secretive. We knew Gram had fallen and was in the hospital and they wouldn't let us kids visit because we might have germs, and that made us mad, too.

I listened through the grate for the particulars, while the others thumped around in the playroom so the grownups wouldn't suspect a spy. Lyman was mad. He wanted to be the spy—but I drew the long straw. I heard Gramp say: "I can take care of her *and* this house." He sounded angry and tired and weak, as though he were the one sick. Through the cast-iron cross-hatch, I could see the top of his lucky bald head; the tremor in his voice reminded me of the way he'd looked a few days earlier, when my brother and I sat at Gram's kitchen table, eating molasses cookies, playing with the salt-and-pepper shakers. I peppered Bert's milk; he salted my cookie. My mother and father talked softly at Gramp across the room. He took off his glasses and set them on the sink counter. I'd never seen him without his glasses. Red sores gleamed where the metal nose-pieces had dug in. The skin around his eyes was bruised and puffy. He looked old.

And he sounded old, as I listened through the fancy cast-

iron grate. He sounded like a weak old man—not my Gramp at
all. "For God's sake, Dad," my mother said, "listen to reason."

They were ganging up on him—my mother and father, the
aunts and uncles; ganging up on him in his own house, and
Gram sick in the hospital so he was feeling bad enough already. I knew how it felt to be ganged up on, because sometimes the cousins ganged up on me and made me do what they
wanted instead of what I wanted, like play King and Queen
instead of Seance. Still, I loved my cousins, who had no choice
but to accept me because we were blood. I loved being among
them at Gram and Gramp's on Sundays and holidays when we
ran amuck, in and out of the house, up and down the stairs,
whispering secrets in the haunted attic, screaming wild horses
across the yard.

The uncles drank cider and played cards or, in summer,
watched the goddamned-Red-Sox on television. The aunts
worked around the kitchen, played board games, sorted their
collections—buttons, postmarks, postcards. Some of them
sipped a little cider, too, but Gram drank only good cold water
to set an example.

These were my perfect days, except when Cousin Lyman
held me by the hair and made me kiss rocks, except when
Cousin Pamela buried my Tammy doll. Perfect days, except
when the time came to pay a duty call on Marymay—also our
blood relation, but a distant one thank God, since nobody really wanted to claim her.

Nobody wanted to visit her either. Still, the grownups would
draw straws, a couple kids would be recruited, a delegation dis-
patched. We'd take an offering of bread or cookies, stay one
hour (or until Marymay let us go), then return to the family
with the taste of licorice tea or stale Canada mints in our
mouths and new Marymay stories to tell:

About how her homemade dresses hung like nightgowns,

the collars basted on, the sleeves different lengths, the hems falling down.

About the rubber raft she mailed away for, blew up by bicycle pump, then tried to paddle through the swamp, only it swamped and she swamped and that was the end of the rubber raft.

About cleaning old hay from the loft, knocking the ladder away when the bat swooped, being stuck up there some hours, darkness, more bats and scurrying things, finally shimmy-jumping down a beam into the pile of debris and breaking just the one small bone.

About shoehorning six cords of wood into the ell, floor to ceiling, a canyon of wood, dangerous to travel through because a chunk might dislodge on your head. (Gramp said a chunk must have already dislodged on Marymay's head, the way she acted. Gram said: "Be kind, Dad.")

About painting the front windows black to prevent the dead-end neighbors from peeking in when they drove by, and, a month later, scraping the paint off to please the philodendron.

About boys sneaking around the barn, looking for trouble. Dangerous boys: Marymay found their spent matches and cigarette butts. They came back several nights in a row, but the last time she was ready for them, hiding behind the millstone.

"With a gun? What'd she do shoot 'em?"

"She flapped an umbrella at 'em. Didn't say a word; just flapped and stared 'em down with her evil eyes. They ran!"

Marymay's eyes were huge, the irises as reflective and variegated as mother-of-pearl. They changed color, but not in the usual way, not because of what she was wearing or the hue of the sky. Color spoke in her eyes. "Don't worry about that old dog," she'd say about the big, nameless dog Lyman claimed was half wolf, half devil. But a wash of purple in Marymay's eyes told us, "Leave it! Or that dog will taste your blood."

"Poor little boys," Gram said. "They must have been scared to death. I'm sure they didn't mean any harm."

"I'm sure they did," Gramp said. "I know those boys. If they come back, they'll probably burn the house down and *her* in it."

"What a thing to say!" Gram said. She warned us to be careful what we predicted because it might come true.

Bert was scared of Marymay and her dog, unapproachable in its shadowy corner. "That dog won't hurt nothing. That dog is as sweet-natured as your Auntie Prill," our father said, but he was a well-known liar.

The dog's eyes were dark but skimmed with milk, and when a child ventured near, its lips would quiver and pull away from its teeth and black gums. "Don't touch the dog," Marymay said. "He's anti-social." Bert thought the dog hated him in particular.

"It's looking at me," he whispered as we shot marbles on the braided rug. We could see the dog between Uncle Judge's boots as he rocked. The marbles didn't roll too well, because the rug was matted with dog hair. Uncle Judge, sensitive to fleas, reached into his sock at regular intervals to scratch. The room was hazy with wood smoke and dust and steam from the licorice tea.

"Don't worry about the dog. The dog's asleep," Marymay said, her eyes tinged jade like carnival glass on the highboy.

"It *is* looking at me," Bert said, and between Uncle Judge's boots, I could see the new-moon glint where the dog's eyelids didn't quite meet.

When the time came each week to choose kids for the delegation, Bert was apt to hide, sometimes in the haunted attic. He felt safer there than at Marymay's. Sometimes we'd find him curled in a corner with one of his little books. "Did Great-Great-Gramma come to see you?" we'd say. "Did she look at you with her white eyes? Did she kiss you with her cold lips? There she is now! She just floated through that wall. She's watching you, Bert." The more we teased and laughed about the ghosts, the more real they became. The ghosts were as real to us as the notion of blood loyalty. They were family and so was Marymay: Do you think we would have bothered with her —crazy old lady—if she hadn't been?

"She's a witch!" Bert said.

"She's not a witch," I said. "She's a Baptist."

I knew this because of the puppets left over from when she used to teach Sunday school. "Let's see if they're awake," she'd say, drawing us into the hall while the grownups gabbed in the plant-jungle parlor. She knelt by the puppet trunk and pulled them out one by one. They smelled of mothballs and smoke and dust. Baby Jesus was wrapped in gauze—he *was* gauze, except for his round wooden head and a pipe cleaner down the middle. But the others wore fancy robes stiffened with brocade and rickrack. "Jesus loves you," she said, poking my neck with John the Baptist's clothespin arm. "Do you know that song, 'Jesus loves the little children'?" Sometimes she sang it, softly, so the grownups wouldn't hear. As she sang, the puppets danced.

The floor grew hard as I lay there spying through the grate, flat on my stomach, the oriental runner itching me through my clothes. Lyman tiptoed out of the playroom—breaking the rule; they were all supposed to stay put; I was the official spy. He tried to sneak up on me, but I felt the vibration of the floorboards. Then he crawled up close and tried to tickle me, but I kicked him and gave him a powerful glare from my own evil eyes. "Get back," I whispered. "They'll hear you." He pinched my leg, retreated and pulled the playroom door almost closed, open just a crack for the others to peek through. All those faces, one on top of the other in the crack, Bert's

round face on the bottom, worried. I motioned for them to
close the door—*close it.* Lyman thumbed his nose, and the
door clicked shut. Then I was alone in the long dark hallway,
except for the ghosts: a chill, a shudder, and I knew one had
brushed me by.

When us kids slept overnight in this house, we heard their
footsteps and faraway voices, in the attic, in the chimney, in
the closet, in the wall, down the hall. Sometimes they tapped
on the windows as though they wanted us to let them in, wan-
derers returning from a ghost walk, tapping on the window to
scare us when they could just as easily melt through. Smart-ass
ghosts. "Just like you, Lyman," I said. "I can tell you're related."
"Just like *you*," Lyman said.

"I don't need any help," I heard Gramp say, "I didn't ask for
your help and I don't need it." But the grownups shouted him
down: Dad, come on, listen to reason. . . . After a while he
stopped talking altogether and the others argued among themselves. My father's voice, breaking in, was so deep I hardly recognized it—my laughing, lying father pretending to be as
grown up as the rest: "Hold on. We don't *know* anything yet.
What's the sense jumping the gun here and getting everybody
worked into a lather?"

My mother said, "Ben, please . . ." like she was already
worked into a lather and Dad better watch out or he'd find
himself in the middle of a big fight because he wasn't blood,
only an in-law, and this wasn't really his business.

Tired of holding up my head, I let my cheek press the cold
metal of the grate, which hurt a little, pinched my ear, and
would leave cross-hatches on my skin, chenille marks, my
mother called them. I rested like that and listened and tried to
understand why they were all so mad at each other, and so
mean to Gramp who had retreated to a corner and was sitting

on the wood box with his head down, studying his hands, his knees, his shoes, the splatterwork linoleum.

Then the telephone rang. It rang six times before anyone stepped forward to answer. The one who finally did pick up the receiver said, "Uh-huh, uh-huh, uh-huh." I think it was Auntie Prill, and I think she said, after she'd hung up and the silence grew long and dense: "She's taken a turn for the worse." At the time I couldn't quite make out the words, or maybe I just didn't understand them because I'd never heard that expression before, but later I figured it out. I think that's what she must have said—but it wasn't so much what she said, as the tone of her voice that made me raise up on my elbows and knees. Kneeling there over the grate, dizzy, still staring down through, I wanted to flee, but the ghosts restrained me. I felt them wrap me in their gauzy arms. I wanted to move, but they wouldn't let go. I felt like Baby Jesus, swaddled in gauze, smothering in it. Then I heard Gramp say in a weak voice, "What am I supposed to do now?"

I don't remember much about running from the house. I don't remember deciding to run. I just did. One moment I was on my knees by the grate, then I was up and thumping down the hall, the playroom door opening wide, but I rushed past. Lyman's face, Bert's face, Pamela and little Sandy and the other cousins wondering "What the hell?"; down over the stairs, out the garden door, across the field and I ended up in the swamp that separated Gram and Gramp's place from Marymay's, my feet sinking in the moss and muck, ferns brushing me, pucker brush poking, clinging and scratching when I pushed through onto the secret path us kids had bushwhacked, to turtle rock and beyond to the double stone wall. I hurtled the stone wall at the place where, if you looked carefully between the two triangle stones, you could see the shape of a deer's head, antlers and all, like a fossil. We said the head was magic and only blood relatives could see it, only blood relatives dared reach in between the two triangle stones and feel how cold and smooth it was.

Once on the other side, I crawled under the limbs of the bull pine, where sometimes, though it was forbidden, us kids hid to spy on Marymay. Though we never saw much, we made much of what we saw: smoke curling from the chimney, swallows nesting in the eaves, the twitch of a curtain, Marymay dumping potato water out the door, ghost shadow passing a window, demon eyes lighting the stained glass at the attic peak.

Breathless, muddy, I curled into a ball on the pine-needley ground, and when, after a while, my breath came back, I listened to it pouring out and in, felt the press of my papery lungs against my ribs. I took in the smell of pine like medicine, because it was familiar and nothing else seemed to be. I mourned the end of perfect days.

A long time later, the dog found me and poked me with its wet nose. I pushed it off, curled up tighter, and covered my ear with my arm.

"Dog," Marymay said, "what are you sniffing at?"

She poked me with her umbrella. "Sleeping on the cold ground gives you hemorrhoids and earaches," she said. "Who is that anyway? Who are you, some trespasser?"

I wanted to say, "Leave me alone!" but I didn't dare—not to a grown-up blood relation, not to a witch, certainly not to a Baptist.

"Get up from that cold ground," she said. I heard her dragging the dog back by the collar. I heard the scratch of earth as toenails dug into the mat of old pine needles. When I peeked out, Marymay had leaned close to inspect me. Her face, framed with evergreen, was huge, her eyes golden.

"Oh, it's you," she said. "What you do, fall down?" I couldn't answer. I'd forgotten how to speak. A breeze blew through the bull pine, and it swished like a whispering congregation.

"The dog wants you to stand up," she said. She brushed pine needles off me. She pulled pine needles out of my hair, and some hair with them. She pulled on my hand, pulled me to my feet, and I had no choice but to walk with her, the dog still sniffing and poking from behind.

Inside, she put the kettle on for tea. The dog and I stood in the middle of the kitchen, watching her. An open jar of grape jelly still on the table from breakfast, an interested fly, a crust of bread like a smile on the sticky plate. "We could get out the marbles," she said. "Or the puppets. Shall we see if they're awake?"

I shook my head.

In the front room, the dog turned three times, then lay down in its corner.

Marymay held out the dish of Canada mints—pink and dusted with white powder. The mint burned my tongue. I let it stay there and melt, hot and grainy. I couldn't swallow. "Sit down," she said. "Your tea will be ready any minute."

I rocked back in the chair, felt the bumps of the crocheted afghan against the back of my head, stared at the ceiling, darkened over the years by wood smoke. There was a patched spot in the ceiling, a squarish gray-blue suture in the plaster, as though a flap had been torn away then sewn back into place, as though the repair had, in fact, been a healing. Marymay said my mother was the one who made that hole in the ceiling, when she was a very little girl, wandering around upstairs like she shouldn't have been on the day the floor was being repaired. She said my mother tried to walk the studs, slipped and fell through. My mother said this never happened except in Marymay's head. Gram said, "I don't remember it. Why, as far as I know that mark on the ceiling has always been there." Last time Marymay told the story about my mother's little feet dangling from the ceiling and the miracle she didn't fall through and break her little neck, my dad said, laughing, "Marymay, you're full of malarkey."

When Marymay returned with the tea, she'd pulled on a moth-eaten cardigan and traded her walking shoes for house slippers. "Your only hope," she said, "is to drink this quick, because you've been lying on the cold ground and that is very bad for your health."

She set my cup and saucer on the wobbly table. "Drink it," she said. My throat felt so tight I thought it might close altogether and suffocate me. I thought the tea might catch halfway down and drown me. "Drink it," she said, her eyes bright as the string of blue bulbs Gram draped across her front porch every year to welcome the family at Christmas. I gulped and choked, but the tea found its slow way down. I drank some more, hot and bitter. Gradually, the light in Marymay's eyes softened, as though the wattage had been reduced. "Finished?" she said.

I held the cup toward her so she could see it was nearly empty. I held it by the handle, carefully because it was old and light, the porcelain very thin. Then I let go. I didn't mean to, but there it was, my fingers suddenly limp, the handle slipping through them, and the precious old cup falling away to the floor. When it hit, it shattered. There was the handle still attached to New Hampshire. There were Maine, Vermont, Massachusetts, and several tiny Rhode Islands. Two many pieces to glue—I could see that at once.

"Oh my," Marymay said. "This *is* a disaster."

She didn't sound angry. She didn't sound hurt. She sounded, almost, cheerful. I flicked a look at her face. She was smiling, a gentle upturn of thin, dry lips. I didn't dare look at her eyes, but I watched, fascinated, as she slowly raised her own cup, the meeting of lips and rim as delicate as a kiss.

"That old thing was chipped anyway," she said. "We're better off without it. The dog certainly thinks so."

The dog shifted in its corner, then settled again, like dust.

I wanted to tell her, I felt I *should* tell her, how things were at the other house. I didn't know, but I *knew*, my Gram was going to die. I was afraid to speak, afraid saying it would make it so, afraid thinking it already had. "I'm sorry," I said to the broken cup. "I didn't mean to."

Then I looked up. I looked into Marymay's eyes and realized I didn't have to say any more. She was still smiling, but her eyes were black and filled with tears.

✠ Peach Baby Food Sandwiches

The idea of peach baby food sandwiches hovered like a cloud of midgies all that long morning fishing. Midgies—those tiny humming bugs too small to swat, so small you hardly feel them biting and so what if they do since it doesn't really hurt. Still, they bother, especially when they come around at night, slide in through the screen and eat you all over in your sleep. Can't get at them, can't get away from them, drive a person wild. And so on this particular day, like a swarm of midgies, the idea of peach baby food sandwiches tormented me—the idea that some time along I might actually have to eat one.

I was out fishing with Pop, who had declined Grammie Dix's funeral: she was no blood relation of his after all. And there was a rule in our family that kids didn't have to go to funerals until they hit double digits. I was only nine.

Fishing Duardo Lake is a tradition in our family. At one time Pop's father, my great-grandfather, owned property on the north shore—where he erected the famous Duardo Lake cross: twenty-five feet tall, hewn of spruce wood, and visible from all over the lake because it was positioned high on the bald-faced lookout. Unlike the Reverend, Pop steered clear of churches. He told me that on Easter Sunday, still, ones from a certain church trooped up to the cross to make holy water, pray for their mortal souls, sing hallelujah, and so forth. He said the lookout was, generally and especially on Easter Sunday, a good place to avoid.

When I looked up at the cross from the middle seat of Pop's old wooden boat, I got a feeling in my stomach—a kind of queasy, uneasy feeling. For a minute I thought I was getting religion. Then I realized probably it was just my subconscious reminding my insides about the peach baby food sandwich with my name on it in the brown paper bag next to the gas can. I prayed for divine intervention—the way Grammie Dix taught me when I stayed over at her house and we watched Billy Graham. *Dear God let the winds come, let a wave crest over this boat, lift that lunch bag up, and carry it away to Kingdom Come.* And, I added, *God-bless-Grammie-Dix-on-her-way-to-heaven-if-there-is-one.*

That morning—in the rush of funeral arrangements, getting me and my equipment to Pop's house, figuring out who was going to ride with who and just where to meet up with the relatives from Vermont—my mother forgot to pack me a lunch. "I don't know where my mind is," she said.

"Don't worry about it," Pop said. "You've got enough on your mind. Shel can eat what I'm eating."

Later, when he said, "I'm eating peach baby food sandwiches today; that sound good to you?" I said I'd never tried one but . . . and he said, "Better than that shit you eat at home —potato chips and candies and grease: I know what you kids eat. Coca-Cola will strip the paint off a Chevrolet and you suck it down like mother's milk. It's a wonder you're not punier than you are. It's a wonder you survive."

I said no more on the subject but watched in quiet horror as he laid out sandwich makings on the scrubbed-pine table. The lid of the Gerber jar popped when he turned it. He spread the mush inside, ghastly orange pulp, thick over slices of Wonderbread. When he pressed the tops into place, the mush oozed out at the edges, too thick to dribble.

Pop, at that time, believed he was suffering from ulcers.

Somebody told him if he ate baby food, his stomach would heal itself. No doctors, no drugs, no surgery: he figured it was worth a try.

He made three sandwiches. Two for him and one for me. He wrapped them neatly in waxed paper, creased the edges, and tucked the folds.

.   .   .

We'd been on the lake an hour or so when we noticed a commotion at the public landing across the way. Some Beaks (what Pop called people from away—I don't know why) were launching an aluminum boat off a trailer. Two men stood in water to their knees; the other shouted orders from the truck cab. I watched them maneuver the boat into the water, then load it with poles, tackle boxes, float cushions, and a white Styrofoam cooler—thankful for the distraction, thankful for a break from Pop's long, hard silences.

One man lost his balance trying to climb in, straddling one foot on a rock and the other in the boat. Looked for a minute like a major spill in the makings, but he lurched forward at last and sprawled across the middle seat. The others were almost as clumsy, waving their arms to save themselves instead of holding steady to the gunnels. When all three were finally settled, the boat rode low—with, it was clear to me, far too little freeboard for safety.

Pop scooped Alpo with two fingers, then trailed his hand through the water until it was clean. Chum. We'd emptied half a can already, without a single bite for our trouble.

"Now what are those jack-asses up to?" Pop pushed his cap back on his forehead. The overloaded Beak boat lugged up the pond in our direction, headed right for us. Acres of fishing spots to choose from and these guys, ignorant of or spurning fishing etiquette, anchored not a hundred feet off our bow.

"Christ Almighty," Pop said.

I shivered. Grammie Dix would have said somebody walked on my grave. Maybe when I died I'd be buried next to Grammie Dix. Maybe all the people at her funeral were right this minute walking on my future grave.

"You cold?" Pop said.

"No," I said.

"You sick?" he said.

"No."

But, of course, I was sick—sick with anticipation because, though I didn't have a watch, I could tell by the sun that the morning was pretty well shot. Approaching noon. Approaching the dreaded lunch hour. Approaching the moment when I would be forced to choose between eating a peach baby food sandwich or . . . not. And, in the case of "not," risking Pop's legendary anger.

The Beak in the khaki vest was red-faced from too much sun or beer or both. He wore a brimmed hat with a large fluorescent fly on the band. Pop named him Mouth because, as soon as the motor quieted and the anchor fed out, he started instructing the others about how to hook the crawler, how many sinkers to squeeze on, which side of the boat to fish from, and so forth. Also, he was bragging about trout he'd caught in the past, how big they were and how many and what an outstanding outdoors man he himself was.

When Mouth hollered over, "How they biting? Any luck?" we pretended not to know he was talking to us—though there were no other boats in shouting distance. We stared at our lines, straight out from the weight of the sinkers, unmoving in water ruffled with a breeze we could not feel. The world shifted when I reached over the side to touch the water. Pop told me to sit still.

As luck would have it, shortly after the Beaks anchored, the fish started to bite. For us anyway. Pop pulled in a ten-incher and was tucking it among wet ferns when I got a hit myself. I set the hook, reeled, felt the weight of the fish still coming, responded to the pull, guided her alongside toward the back of the boat where Pop scooped her in the net. Not quite the size of Pop's, but respectable, edible. I turned my back to the Beaks to re-bait with three slippery red salmon eggs. Lesson number one: never let the other guy know what you're fishing with. Pop had already re-baited fast and in the palm of his hand—like a magician doing a coin trick. He slid hook-line-and-sinker back under water in the blink of an eye—no Beak the wiser.

"What you catch those on?" Mouth yelled.

I looked at Pop, my breath stuck in my throat. This was a serious breach and I thought Pop might just erupt on the spot. Where did these people come from that they didn't know not to ask *that* question of a fisherman?

Maybe Boston, I thought. I'd heard people from Boston were half-crazed with pollution and overcrowding. I'd heard Boston streets were so windy, criss-crossed, and full of speeding cars that a traveler couldn't get his bearings. I'd heard there were criminals in Boston who would poke revolvers through your window when you stopped for a red light, that these criminals would pound your car, smash your lights, call you names, rob you and/or kill you without a second thought. Sometimes on our once-a-year trip to Manchester Christmas shopping, we'd see the highway sign that said Boston and pointed south. "Don't go that way, Bob," my mother'd say. "My God, turn off quick or we'll end up in *Boston,*" giving me the feeling that if we didn't turn off in time, if through some miscalculation or misfortune we ended up on I-93, southbound—well, it would be all over for us. We'd be pulled by some irresistible force—like gravity, only horizontal— right into the heart of the city: and there—being innocent country folk from New Hampshire—we would certainly be abused, ridiculed, assaulted, and lost forever.

Yes, it seemed clear: the Beaks were Bostonians—out of their element, confused, perhaps lost themselves. Could they really be blamed for their ignorance after all?

"What you got there," Mouth said. "Something in that little jar?"

On another day, in a better mood, Pop might have told some outrageous lie and laughed at them—but not on this day. His rich voice carried over the water, each word fully formed and distinct. "What we're using for bait," he said, "happens to be none of your goddamned business."

The Beaks pretended to laugh. But I could tell they didn't think it was funny. Neither did we. Shortly after that, they hauled anchor and tooled down the pond and around the bend —leaving us rocking in their wake.

I sat there in the blessed quiet that followed, trying to control my rumbling stomach. By moving just right when a rumble started, I could settle it quick, hide the sound with the shush of my butt across the plank seat.

Pop said: "Hungry?"

I said: "Big breakfast."

Pop said: "Well then, this hole seems about fished out—we might as well troll, see if we can't scare up a little something in the cove."

He pull-started the Evinrude, adjusted it low, and set us on course. I half-hitched a wet fly to the monofilament on the trolling pole, then let out three colors of lead line, and propped the pole across my knees.

"I'm not hungry yet," I said over the putt-putt of the motor.

Pop handed me a sandwich, an apple, and a bottle of grape soda.

"I am," he said.

We were moving so slow and smooth that he could eat, steer, keep the throttle even, and watch me at the same time. I wedged the soda between my legs, stuffed the apple in my mouth, and laid the sandwich, still wrapped, on the seat beside me. He held the steer bar with one hand; his sandwich, thermos cup, and apple alternately with the other. He took big bites and small swigs. I ate the apple too fast and tossed the core. His deep-set eyes were intensely blue—the blue of my father's eyes turned up a notch, the blue of my own eyes times three. He seemed to be studying my face—in particular, the mole at the curve of my left nostril. I popped the top off the soda bottle with the opener on my survival knife and took a long drink.

I unwrapped the peach baby food sandwich. It lay on the waxed paper limp as a hankie. Pop's eyes narrowed as we headed into the sun, water sparkling like diamond necklaces strung out shore to shore. I could barely make out the silhouette of the Beak boat rocking toward the middle of the broads. Pop steered clear of that irritation, heading—I knew—for the far cove where on a warm afternoon, the monsters down deep might strike the right wet fly trolled at the right speed, right depth.

I nudged apple peel from between my teeth with my thumbnail. Pop smacked his lips over the last bite of his first sandwich, wiped the back of his hand across his mouth, sniffed the breeze created by the motion of the boat. He was still watching me, from the corner of his eye, expectant. I picked up my sandwich, nibbled the edge—where I thought it was bread only, but some of the peach mush touched my tongue. God—it was like eating puke.

"What's the matter," he said.

"Nothing," I said.

I laid the sandwich down on the waxed paper and considered my options. If I threw the sandwich in the water, it would float. Having fed many ducks in my time, I knew it would float. Pop would see it floating by. If I broke it into tiny pieces, they would float too. Pop would see them floating. He'd know exactly what they were. He'd know exactly what I'd done. There had to be another way.

He pulled the steer bar sharply, the sandwich slid across the seat and lodged against my knee. In this cove, the bottom dropped off fast. Sometimes the big rainbows congregated where feeder springs bubbled up. I knew he was planning to troll across the drop-off in an attempt to attract a big one with his modified Homburg dragged at just the right speed, just the right depth.

The trees grew bigger after the turn, the bushes along the shore came into focus, and all at once a plan took shape in my mind. I realized that in this swing through the cove we would pass so close to shore that a person with a strong arm and good aim could toss a sandwich in behind the chokecherry bushes, in behind the fringe of hemlock. I realized that tossed just so, a sandwich would virtually disappear. I embraced hope.

"Look Pop," I said, pointing behind us at nothing in particular, figuring he'd find something to interest him, being a curious, sharp-eyed outdoors man like he was. There was the Beak boat away out in the middle with one foolish Beak standing up, casting for God's sake, the boat tipping crazily with each swing of his arm. There was a pair of red-tailed hawks, circling. And behind them on the cliff—evidence of the divine intervention I'd prayed for—was the famous Duardo Lake cross lit up like glory—as it was apt to be, on a bright day when the sun struck at just the right angle and the wood shone like steel or like somebody'd flipped on a light inside. *God-bless-Grammie-Dix,*

I thought, *on-her-way-to-heaven-which-I-think-there-probably-is-one*.

Pop turned. He had to turn clear around to see all that I had seen.

At that precise moment—his broad back to me, his head cranked way around—I saw my chance and took it. I hurled that peach baby food sandwich as hard as I could toward shore. The boat rocked. The sandwich arced beautifully, held itself together and soared toward the bushes. As it soared, I felt relief all over, believing the sandwich was on its way to a permanent resting place—no Pop the wiser.

But . . .

A dead, sun-bleached, leaning hulk of a tree I hadn't even noticed until the sandwich was airborne stuck out a long, brittle, pick-ed branch—and that sandwich, just at the crest of its beautiful arc, impaled itself.

There it hung.

Pop turned to me, his hand firm on the steer bar, the boat moving as slowly as I have ever known it to move, the motor revving just a notch above stall. He said: "Those damn-fool Beaks, standing up in that boat. They'll tip themselves over for sure."

The sandwich now hung directly over his head, about eight feet up. I could feel a breeze rising.

He said: "God knows they'll probably drown themselves and we'll end up having to haul out their dead carcasses."

"I think they're from Boston," I said, expecting the breeze to tear the sandwich free, bracing for the moment the sandwich fell smack on Pop's head.

He leaned forward to grab the waxed paper which now threatened to blow out of the boat. He crumpled it, tucked it in the brown paper bag, tucked the brown paper bag under the tackle box.

And all at once we were out from under the overhanging branch, out from under the telltale sandwich, and moving slowly through the cove. Slowly. Pop pulled his pipe from his shirt pocket, filled it, and lit up. I watched the smoke as it spiraled from the pipe and trailed over his shoulder. His lips looked soft and strangely pink, pursed around the black pipe stem.

I tried not to stare where I shouldn't be staring, but couldn't help myself, because there it hung just a few yards back, the biggest peach baby food sandwich ever created by God or man —and it seemed to be expanding. Unnaturally white and square and huge, it seemed impossible to miss. I imagined the Beaks, clear across the pond, discussing it: "What's that big white thing up in the tree? See it over there. Is that a flag or something? Somebody's underwear maybe?" If Pop twitched an inch to the right, if he cocked his good eye eastward, if he turned for one last check on the Beak boat or a glimpse of the Duardo Lake cross, he couldn't miss it.

"Pop . . ." I don't know what I was going to say. Certainly not "I cannot tell a lie. I didn't eat my sandwich—look for yourself, it's in that tree behind you." Still, I wanted to confess. The punishment couldn't be worse than the tension of wondering when the ax (or, in this case, the sandwich) would fall. I imagined the splash, loud as a rainbow doing a belly flop.

Pop's eyes held mine so hard I couldn't blink. My mouth went dry as crackers. He stared into my brain; he knew everything there was to know about me—every lie I'd ever told. His yellow teeth bit down hard on the pipe stem as he shaped words of doom. "We'll motor on down shore a ways," he said. "And then we'll circle around for one more swing through the cove."

The cold sweat started then—seeping, it felt like, from every pore. Dizzy, I blinked to clear my eyes, fogged and stinging from the sweat waterfall off my forehead. I looked again where

I shouldn't have been looking, behind Pop, beyond him. I blinked to focus on what had to be an optical illusion—though I didn't think so at the time, though sometimes, even now, I'm not altogether sure. Maybe I was crazed with fear, weak from hunger, and sun-struck, too, but as I stared at that peach baby food sandwich, unable to see anything else, before my eyes it transformed—elongating, separating itself into four clearly defined fingers and a thumb. I caught the golden glint of a wedding band and, at the wrist, the shadow of a ruffled sleeve.

And then it waved at me, to me. Bye-bye, Shel, bye-bye: the friendly, dancing fingers of a dead old lady's hand—unmistakable against a sky as alarmingly blue as my grandfather's eyes.

⚏ Parasites

"Sorry I'm late," I tell my two-o'clock class. "Family emergency."

I'm not *that* late—but they were about to bolt. Brats.

Van strolls in behind me, also late. Unapologetic. Van-the-beautiful, the center of his own universe.

My husband Michael says Van and I have a personality conflict.

Correct.

Poor Van—he doesn't know I'm going to nail him before the day is out.

Michael will be proud.

He's always said I let my students get away with too much. "They're just little kids, really," I'd insist. "Away from home, under a lot of pressure, confused. They could use a little nurturing."

Except Van.

"Touchy-feely," says Michael the hard ass. "This is the university—not kindergarten."

"Stuff it," I say.

"Give no A's, no extensions, no special consideration. Take no flak; take no prisoners."

"You teach your way, Michael; I'll teach mine."

He's teaching his way in London for the semester—an opportunity not to be missed. "Go," I said. "Laura and I will be fine. Our love will survive. Don't think a thing about it."

Pretty mature attitude, wouldn't you say?

Don't think a thing about it, Michael.

It's just a small case of plagiarism and I have no proof. Just a little lice infestation and Laura out of school and I have no baby-sitter. Just the year I'm up for tenure—thumbs up/thumbs down, baby. Just the occasional blinding migraine.

. . .

In Michael's entomology book, saved from his undergraduate years, three pages are devoted to parasitic lice. "Lice live in the skin world and enjoy the bounty of flakes and sebaceous exudates," it says.

A lyrical text.

Clearly the writer is devoted to her subject.

"Look, Laura." I slide her onto my lap. "This is a picture of a louse."

It's a full-page, black-and-white photo of a louse magnified eighty times—aerial view. The body is short, wide, pale as a maggot. Two segmented pincers stretch forward, menacing, glowing at the tips. Six sturdy legs splay. On the body, fine white hairs, sparse and random, and stubs that suggest wings lost to evolution.

"Mommy!" Laura wails, and she tries to slam the book shut, but my hand is in the way and she's squishing it.

"Laura," I wail. "It's just bugs. Nothing to be upset about, nothing to be embarrassed about. It's just little bugs. Some bugs live in the garden. Some bugs live in your hair."

"Don't talk about it!" she says.

. . .

Van is a communications major who aspires to be a television anchorman. He looks the part: beautiful gray eyes, straight-across brows, square teeth and chin. His chestnut hair is pulled into a neat ponytail at the nape of his neck. He radiates intelligence—something in the eyes, not a sparkle exactly, but a certain alertness.

He looks bright. He's not. He needs to pull at least a B in this course. It's a prerequisite.

"Uh, Linda," he says. "I signed up a conference, but I can't make it." He shrugs.

"You can't make it? I rearranged my schedule to fit you in and you can't make it?"

"I can't make it."

"Then we have a problem."

"I don't have a problem," he says.

He takes a step toward me. We are side-by-side facing the impatient class.

He drapes his arm loosely across my shoulders. "Whatever you say, Teach."

I stiffen and contract.

He removes his arm, slowly, the rough knit of his sweater catching my hair, raising the hackles on my neck. Someone snickers. Van takes his usual seat with his back to the window, the sun haloing his head.

. . .

"He hates you," Michael said the third week of the semester, when I shared a few choice Van stories long distance. "He's hostile."

"No kidding."

"Kick him out of your class. You don't have to put up with that."

"Put up with what—laughing behind my back, a few wise-cracks, his disconcerting glare. I think I do have to put up with it, until he crosses the line. Maybe, once he gets to know me, once he gets into the writing—"

"Watch your back," Michael said. "Get him before he gets you."

.   .   .

A female louse lays ten eggs a day and will lay for up to a month. That's three hundred eggs. Half the hatchlings, being female, will also lay ten eggs a day. In three months, a little girl's head can become a louse metropolis.

The school nurse explained that Laura's lice had reached the crawling stage, indicating a long-term infestation, weeks of infestation, perhaps months.

I hadn't noticed.

She didn't seem that itchy.

I thought it was dandruff.

I stared at Nurse Cote's taut profile, the blond fuzz at her jaw line, the curve of her earring, three shades pinker than her pink cheeks, like a dollop of cake frosting clipped to her lobe.

"Look," she said, parting Laura's hair with a jumbo Q-tip and tilting the fluorescent lamp. Laura sniffled. "See right there," the nurse said, handing me the magnifying glass. "There's a cluster of eggs. And there's a live one! Did you see it?"

I saw it.

"She'll have to be removed from school," the nurse said, "and she can't come back until we're sure the lice and eggs are all dead."

Would I have to produce death certificates? Collect the corpses?

"These kids put their heads together," she said, "and the lice have a field day. Before you know it the whole class is infested and they're just passing them back and forth and all I do all day is check heads. It's horrendous."

My head started to itch, but I didn't scratch it. Didn't want to give Attila-the-nurse any ideas. She had enough problems.

Don't we all.

Michael's book says the optimum temperature for head lice is 87°F. Lice can't survive on a corpse, because the temperature of a corpse's skin world is too low. When a host dies, lice seek new digs.

If I were dead, I'd be all set.

. . .

"It's clear this guy has a thing about women in positions of power," Michael said.

"Like me?"

"He's goading you."

"Tell me about it."

"Be careful, or he'll turn the whole class against you. I've seen it happen."

"He comes to class late, leaves early, complains about assignments, says I'm prejudiced against frat-boys like him, says I'm prejudiced and subjective, says I grade on the amount of spilled guts on the page. 'Linda, you must like that story,' he says, 'the grandmother dies. You like it when they die. Too bad all my grandparents are still alive. I'll never pull an A.' That's for sure. He pretends he's being funny. He thinks he's funny. The rest of the class thinks he's funny. At my expense."

"And you let him get away with it?"

In the skin world—as opposed to the worlds of, say, thought, relationships, emotions—life must be wonderfully simple. A louse sucks blood, mates, lays eggs, takes a ride on a woolly sweater, lays some more eggs, munches sebaceous exudates, and then she dies.

Sounds good to me.

During class, my miserable little itchy-headed daughter waits in my office, tucked away with books, crayons, drawing paper, snacks, her favorite rubber lizard and instructions to stay put.

I hope she's staying put.

I hope she's not wandering the halls in search of the bathroom or a candy machine, dispersing lice as she goes. I picture her pushing into a crowd, a louse leaping onto a professor's tweed elbow. I picture a concerned co-ed, somebody's big sister, bending down—"Are you lost?"—a strand of co-ed hair falling forward, mingling with Laura's, a strategically positioned louse seizing opportunity by beginning the long, slippery climb toward the co-ed's hospitable scalp.

. . .

Twenty-six years ago, when I was in first grade, Warren Crisp got lice. He was pulled out of class and sent home. When he returned, a week later, he was bald!

The older kids invented a game: "Crispy cooties, no returns." And they played it sometimes right in front of him and made him cry. They pretended to pull lice out of one another's hair and eat them. They'd smack their lips. "Crispy," they'd sing.

My mother told me not to catch cooties, in the same tone and with the same implied threat with which she told me not to lie, steal, pick my nose, swear, eat dirt, or beat up my sister Sheila. A good girl wouldn't get cooties, but a bad girl might, and a bad girl would be punished. I know how to avoid lying, stealing, picking my nose, swearing, eating dirt, beating up Sheila. But I didn't know how to avoid cooties. They were fast (I'd heard). They could fly (I'd heard) and were practically invisible. I avoided Warren Crisp, which was hard because he loved me and wanted to marry me when we grew up.

But what if someone else had cooties and I didn't know it and I caught them by mistake? God, what if I caught cooties and got pulled out of school just like Warren Crisp. What if I turned up bald?

.   .   .

Class is over. The hall fills. "We have a problem, Van." I've caught him at the door.

He pushes a loose strand of hair behind his ear. Movie-star hair, thick, full of body, aglow with highlights. I am reminded of the young Lauren Bacall, her hair falling like a curtain over one beautiful eye. "You need a conference, *today*, Van. We need to find a time. How about now?"

"I don't need—"

"I need to see you today."

"You need me, huh?"

Silence.

"I got a class, now," he says.

"After that?"

"I got a lab."

"After that?"

"What is this about, Linda? What's the big deal if I miss one lousy conference?"

"Excuse me?"

"Not that I don't learn a lot. Not that I don't really *enjoy* having you tear my papers to shreds."

"Let's say 7:15, Van, in my office. Bring your notes and your drafts of the last paper you turned in. You did save your drafts?"

"No . . ."

"No?"

"I used my roommate's word processor. It's a first draft . . ."

"Doesn't read like a first draft."

"I mean I didn't print all the million other drafts out. I worked hard on it. Yes, I did. Real hard, Teach."

"Don't call me that. It's inappropriate and it's not funny."

He opens his mouth. Closes his mouth.

"Just bring whatever you have, Van." I smile.

. . .

I pressed Laura's head to my chest. Her hair smelled of Exterminite, guaranteed (if applied thoroughly and at proper intervals) to stop lice in their six-legged tracks.

"I'm going to comb your hair now," I said. "I have to use this tiny comb to get all the eggs off before your hair dries."

"No! It hurts."

"I haven't even started yet. How can it hurt?"

"No," she said, squirming.

"Yes," I said.

. . .

Van tilts back in the wooden chair, the planes of his face illuminated by the green light from my brass desk lamp. His eyes are shadowed. His ponytail curls like a well-groomed rodent on his shoulder. He clasps his hands behind his head and stretches his legs until the tip of one athletic shoe touches my ankle. I cross my legs, re-orient my chair, bend over his paper on the desk.

Van digs into his backpack. "I threw most of the drafts away," he says. "But this one, I found in the trash." It is crumpled and stained. He smoothes it out on the desk. "I didn't know we had to keep drafts."

"It's in the syllabus," I say.

My head itches. Under cover of my hair, I scratch the itchiest spot with the nail of my little finger. "Van, is there something you want to tell me?"

He looks straight into my eyes. "Huh?"

. . .

Pile bedding waist high in the living room. Quarantine eighty-eight stuffed animals in sealed plastic garbage bags in the garage. Spray Habitat Exterminite on the pillows, the upholstery, the rugs, the mop boards. Inhale toxic fumes. Invite migraine. Vacuum the lice-harboring dust from every crack. Scrub with bleach and water. Move big furniture seeking dust kitties and hair balls as Laura huddles in front of the T.V.—a catatonic little ball—watching her *Flight of Dragons* tape: dragons in danger as washer and dryer intone Gregorian chants. Disinfect the cat: cat-scratch six inches long on my forearm. *God damn cat.*

. . .

"You used some interesting language in your paper, Van." I plant my elbows on the desk pad, cat scratch red as a tattoo, twisted like a vine. "You show a remarkable range of vocabulary."

"Thanks."

"What exactly does 'supine' mean?"

"You're the English teacher."

"You used the word. You must know what it means."

He looks away. He studies the poster over my desk: sensuous green peppers, the intriguing interplay of shadow and light. A bead of clear liquid forms half in and half out of Van's left nostril. It hangs there. He doesn't sniff. The green peppers take on monstrous proportions. I can hardly bear to look at them, so I pick up a pen and circle words on his first page: aesthetic, parsimonious, reciprocity.

I push the page toward him and scratch behind my left ear.

"Do you know what the punishment for plagiarism is at this university?"

I lean forward into the light, fold my hands on his paper. His eyes slide over mine. I study the canyon between my thumbnail and the flesh of the thumb itself. I see a speck, smaller than a flea and maggot-white. I look for legs and pincers but the details blur. The insect is tiny as a poppy seed, alive and kicking in the struggle to free itself from the vice of nail and flesh.

Michael said, "Maybe he plagiarized because he's hostile. Or maybe he's hostile because he plagiarized."

Or maybe he hates me because I'm me. And maybe he plagiarized because he's stupid and immoral.

I want him out of my class and my life. Like the singing nurse in *South Pacific*, I want to wash this boy right out of my hair.

I insert the nail of my index finger under my thumbnail and squash the louse. It is surprisingly soft—not hard like a flea, but soft like a mosquito.

"You know it's against the law to accuse somebody of something they didn't do. I could sue you," Van says. "You don't have any proof."

"Yes, I do," I lie.

I'm impatient to get home. There's laundry to fold. A child

to tuck in. A letter to Michael that needs writing: Who says I'm too easy on students, hard ass?

"Do you want to end this here, in this office, between ourselves? Or do you want me to go to the Dean? You can take the F for the course, or I'll call the Dean right now. You know you can be expelled for cheating."

"I don't believe this," he says.

"That's the deal, Van. Take it or leave it."

.   .   .

I lean in my doorway to monitor his exit from the building. I want him good and gone. Arrogant son-of-a-plagiarist!

I consider, briefly, calling him back as he strides down the long, dimly lit hall, as he glides under the stately plaster arch. A more nurturing person might call the boy back. A more compassionate person might warn him that when he tipped back the chair in my small office, when he rested his beautiful head against my coat hung from the wall hook; or earlier, when he put his arm around me in class, when he brushed his prickly sweater against my hair, on any of those occasions, he might have attracted a louse — or two.

⚑ Etta Walks

When Etta looks across the ravine, she sees columns of frozen smoke: white-gray columns, each a foot or more through, some straight, some swirled between ground and sky. Smoke from campfires long extinguished. Smoke trapped in a pocket of impossible cold and impossibly frozen there in the woods.

She stands transfixed on the path she's created with her own walking. On thaw days she left footprints in the softened soil under the leaves and pine needles; then came the freeze and the footprints stayed. She walks every day, often several times a day, over the weeks, now months, since the miscarriage.

She knows neighbors ask sometimes how she is coping. Her mother and father tell them—"Oh, she's doing all right. She's getting along." They expect her to be as resilient as they are. And the neighbors say, "That's fine. Fred and Etta are young and healthy—just starting out. They've got time."

If neighbors ask Fred how she is doing, he says: "Etta walks." She's heard him say this, from the other room when she isn't supposed to be listening, when the neighbors pause at the door, reluctant to leave without reassurance. But Fred doesn't lie to spare other people's feelings. He knows that Etta walks daily and for miles through the woods—never along the road. He doesn't know why, or whether this is a good sign or bad. He knows only that in this way and others her routine has changed, their lives have changed, his wife has changed.

"What's wrong?" he says when she turns away from him in

bed and lies, back to him, curled in on herself. He thinks of
fiddlehead ferns, curled tight. "What's wrong?" when she sits
too quiet at the breakfast table. Then she turns hurt eyes upon
him—how could you ask such a question?—a silent little ghost
who sips scalding tea and watches him eat the warm, sticky
oatmeal she prepares but won't eat herself.

Down at the barn—Fred's thoughts drowning in the hiss of
the milking machine, the moaning of the cows—her father
might ask about things in his matter-of-fact way—"Etta busy
puttering around the house these days? Her mother hasn't seen
much of her. Spring cleaning, huh?" or "What's her plan for
going back to work? I imagine she'll be going back soon"—
both men averting their eyes, studying damp concrete, beads
of condensation on stainless steel. Etta has been an aide at the
elementary school for three years. She talked about going back
to college, finishing her degree, getting certified to teach.
Working on the farm has never been enough for her. Fred's
answer to Etta's father might be a shrug. Or, simply, "I don't
know." Or, on a day when he feels particularly miserable—when her misery becomes his, though he tries to ignore
it: "I couldn't tell you. I wish the hell I could." Or, on a day
following a sleepless night when he fantasizes separation, then
divorce, starting fresh: "Understand *this* about your daughter:
she does what she wants to do."

.   .   .

Etta sees columns of frozen smoke and knows the world across
the ravine is not her world at all but a different place—like
Middle Earth, Narnia, or Eden—where the laws of nature are
modified or suspended. She stands on the path her own walking has created, reluctant to leave it, but drawn by her vision.

She is not afraid. She can't remember ever having been

afraid in these woods. When she was a child she dreamed escape here. In those days people believed in UFOs—and because they believed, they saw them: like stars but brighter and
moving; like satellites but erratic, back and forth across the sky,
then disappearing; like meteors shooting up instead of down.
When a square of ice melted for no reason in the middle of
their neighbor's farm pond, the government investigated. Lo-
cals took chainsaws to the ice and peeled it away while the
government men in long dark coats stood along the shore
watching.

But they found nothing unusual down below. Just stumps
and stones and an old car chassis.

As a child, Etta worried that a UFO really had caused the
melting of the ice. She grew afraid of aliens. She closed the
curtains on the window by her bed. She slept under three blankets and a quilt with the pillows over her head, hiding. But in
dreams, when they came for her with their bright lights, she
ran to safety out the back door, through the apple orchard,
leaping the wire fence and on into the woods where no one
would ever find her.

After all, no one had found her great-grandmother when she
walked away. This was the family story—and true: Grammie
Rosa knew the woods better than anyone because she picked
wild herbs, scraped spruce gum, and dug ginseng root in secret
places. Grammie Rosa was strong and independent. She swore
she'd never be a burden to her family. She also swore she'd
never leave the farm.

When the time came, she said, when old age or sickness
caught up to her, she would walk away while she was still able,
and they'd never find her.

In fact, she did walk away one afternoon when the leaves
were falling, but surprising heat made the world golden, like
summer come again. And though the whole town searched,

they found nothing. After that, the big woods between the farm and the river were called Rosa's.

In her childhood fantasies and even now as a grown woman, Etta meets destiny in Rosa's woods—face to face on a secret path. I'm Etta, she'd say, and extend a hand.

.   .   .

After all this safe time of walking so carefully in her own footprints, Etta now walks new ground, down the hill into the ravine, the layers of half-frozen leaves slick under her boots. She steps stone to stone across the brook, though the ice is still in place, white and growing punky. Then she pulls herself up the other side—too steep to walk—clutching tree trunks for balance, and on toward the columns of frozen smoke which must be farther away than they look, because the more she walks, the more they seem to recede.

The hemlock, prickly on her face, isn't nearly as thick up close as it looked from far away. The sharp pine scent strikes her and then she is through. Where the land flattens out, she stumbles over a meadow of stones—stones plowed up long ago, she guesses, and gathered for a wall no one ever built. Most of the stones are a foot or more across, some rounded, some angular, some sharp. Walking on them is difficult, even dangerous —easy to turn an ankle or stub a toe and go down hard. Maybe they are markers deliberately arranged. She thinks of UFOs hovering, singeing the stones with gases that let the ships down easy. She thinks of the standing stones that protect ancient Celtic fortresses, an army of vertical stones making the ground too rough for an enemy to approach with any speed on horseback or even on foot. These are not standing stones, but lying-down stones; in summer they would be camouflaged by poison ivy. She can see the tough, bare vines weaving through.

She kneels, in spite of the poison ivy, to test the stones. They are not frozen into the ground because there is no ground to freeze to, just another layer of stone beneath the first, and another, and another. Stones all the way down. She walks the perimeter and sees how the juniper grows to the edge, but no further; how the thick, pale tree roots reach in but, finding nothing to sustain them, curl away again. She studies the lay of the stony land.

She's read of children slipping through unbelievably small openings into old wells or pipes or caverns where, say, a mass of tree root had rotted away, leaving a cavity. The hole she discovers among the stones seems too small even for a child, and yet . . . She lifts a stone to enlarge the hole. The stone seems light, hollow. She tosses it aside, then lifts another and another.

She stares down into the darkness, knowing from its intensity that the hole must be very deep. Now the opening is large enough for her to reach in, or crawl through, or slide through—the ledge she's uncovered forms a kind of slide, almost, but not quite perpendicular—inviting her to take a ride.

She knows at once this is Rosa's place. She knows that somewhere, within, lie Rosa's bones and the pistol that came up missing after Rosa had gone.

Etta sits on the edge of the cavern she has uncovered with her own hands, her legs touching the darkness. She feels as though her legs are submerged in something other than air, thicker, warm and tempting. *How deep is this lake*, she wonders, *this lake of stone?*

She pictures Rosa's old bones—skull and spine, femur and fingers. Some would be thick as tree roots. All would be white as milk quartz, but not so hard. Breakables, her mother would call them, like Rosa's bone china, relegated forever to the back of the china closet, kept away from the children so it could be passed on to them.

Would Rosa's bones be lined up as properly as that china—the knee bone connected to the leg bone, the ankle bone connected to the foot bone, the tea cup prim on its saucer? Would the fingers curve over the butt of the pistol? Would the pistol be rusted? Would it still be loaded?

I'm sitting on Rosa's grave, she thinks, *and I'm the only one who knows.*

The only one.

The only one who walks the path her own walking created. The only one who saw, from that path, the impossible columns of frozen smoke. And, lured by them, the only one who knows what it is to be Etta in this strange place.

When Fred asks "What's wrong?" he means "How long?" How long will it take for her to go on, as he has. To him, the curve in her back, the bulge in her stomach, the twinges, the heartbeat had never been a child. Just a fetus. Deformed, they said. Non-viable, they said. All for the best.

Etta pulls her feet from the hole and stretches out on the stony ground. She lies flat on her stomach. She pokes her head in as far as she can. She breathes deep, feeling the expansion of her chest against a ridge of stone. She stretches her arms, her wrists, her long fingers far into the darkness. She imagines hands reaching toward hers, desperate for a touch. She stretches a little farther, the toes of her boots wedged.

"My baby had a name," she whispers.

So did I.

"My baby's name was Sandra," she says.

I know.

Etta pulls back then with an instinct strong as dropping the pan that sears your palm. Up on her feet and running—the tears wet her face as she crosses the rough stone. She tears through the hemlock. She slides down one side of the ravine, crackles the ice on the brook, scrambles up the other side. Not until she is back on her path, standing on ground she has molded to the contours of her own feet, does she stop and look back.

Standing there, gasping each breath, air too thin, too cold, painful going down. She thinks perhaps she never left this path in the first place. She sees again the white-gray columns of frozen smoke. She feels their pull. But even in Etta's world, smoke cannot freeze. She peels her tears away. And when she looks again, she sees that the columns were not smoke at all, only birch trees changed by the light.

⊯ Walking the Trapline

My brother Thomas's snowshoes were bigger than mine, though he was smaller than me. Father made the snowshoes. It took a long time because the ash for the frames had to be aged and steamed into shape. The deer hide had to be soaked in the brook until the hair floated off and then tanned in our cellar. One year the neighbor's dog dragged the hide out of the brook and chewed it. Father saw the tracks. He found the ruined hide. Later, he shot the dog. I think the neighbors knew, but they never said so.

On winter evenings, Father sliced the stiff hides into strips to soak in coffee cans until they were supple and slimy. He knotted them to the frames. His big, scarred hands squeaked each strand tight and even into place.

The small finger on his right hand was a shiny stub. The beaver trap had "snipped the little feller right off," he said, when he told the story. But I remembered the bloody mitten.

Father cut my leather harnesses plenty big for me to grow into. When the insides were webbed, dried, and varnished over, he sliced the harnesses thick and measured them to my feet. As he knelt to adjust the buckles around my rubber boots, I saw his pale scalp through the thinning curls.

He was a young father just the same, with a hard jaw, all his front teeth, and blue eyes that made me feel dirty when he stared at me. Mother said I had eyes like my father and asked what I was staring at all the time. She never asked him.

When I was eleven and Thomas was nine, Father began to teach him about the trapline. He allowed me to come along when the weather was fine and the dishes done.

Father trapped beaver through the ice, mink in the brooks, and fisher in the trees. He got good money for the pelts. He said his job at the tannery, which made him smell so sour, wouldn't be enough to feed us if it weren't for the animals he caught.

When Mother complained that he ought to be tending to the woodpile or the roof or the broken cellar steps, he'd say he trapped for the money and she should be glad. She'd stare him in the eye just a second till her face had to twitch away. She knew he trapped because he wanted to, and that was all.

He tended the sets he had to drive to in the evenings after work. On Sundays, he made the rounds of the traps in the big woods out behind our house.

"Do you think we'll catch anything today?" I asked, snow-shoeing behind him and Thomas up the hill behind our house. The snow was new and light and clean. It barely held the imprint of my webbing.

"Your mother would rap me a good one if I came back with nothing, Elizabeth."

I laughed. She would never rap him, though she might get cross and not make supper if she thought he had wasted the whole day. When she did not make supper, Thomas and I went to our room early to get away from her silence.

I liked to step on the tails of Thomas's snowshoes and make him stumble when we walked downhill. Sometimes he'd stumble too far and jar Father. "Watch it, boy," Father would growl. And Thomas would look back at me real ugly.

"You see those tracks down over that banking?" Father stopped so quick I almost walked over Thomas.

"Yup," I replied.

"You see them swish marks and how square they are?"

"Yup," I replied. I could have told him what kind they were, but he always finished a lesson once he started it.

"A little female fisher," he said. "She's moving on a new snow. We might get up here a-ways and find her hanging in my little trap."

"I hope so," I said.

Father stared at Thomas until he looked up. "Wouldn't that be dandy, boy?"

Thomas nodded.

I curled my thumbs in my mittens. Mid-morning by the sun, and the air was still cold enough to stiffen the skin in my nose.

We found the trap empty and sprung. The bait was gone. Father picked up a feather. "Sprung by a Christly blue jay. Fisher come along, just climbed right up and ate that bait slick as a bean." He stomped the feathers into the snow. Thomas and I stood silent and close together, elbows rubbing. Better not make matters worse, we thought. Thomas and I thought about some things the same way. We'd catch one another's eye and understand we were thinking and feeling the same.

"She'll be back," Father said.

"She'll be back," I said to Thomas, who knew as well as I did that fisher travel in circles and always come back.

Father pulled the pack basket off his back as if it wasn't heavy a bit. He laid it up against the leaning birch tree beside the ice chisel he carried like a staff. My father was strong. When the beaver trap sprung on one hand, he opened it with the other to free himself.

"Can we build a fire?" Thomas asked.

"What, you cold?"

"No." Thomas was shivering. I kicked him in the ankle, meaning "Tell him you're cold." Thomas knew what I meant, but clamped his mouth shut. He could be stubborn about things that didn't count.

"I'm cold," I said. It was all right for me to be cold.

Father didn't hear.

Thomas and I played tag to keep warm and threw snow at one another because we liked to. We were careful not to throw snow at Father. When he played snow fight, he'd run us down one at a time and rub our faces with snow.

"You kids get away from this set if you're going to raise hell," he said.

I sat by the pack, tired of the game anyhow. Thomas walked away.

"Reach in that bag and find my bottle of scent, Elizabeth." Father's scents were secret. He said they were made of deer glands, skunk juice, fish oil, and other secret things that no other trappers could know and we must never tell.

He had strung up the new piece of beaver carcass. He plucked a branch of hemlock and wired it over the meat—to make it look natural, he said. Fisher didn't know hemlock branches did not grow on birch trees.

Father didn't catch many fisher in a season; there weren't too many around. I had never seen one in a trap, only in the cellar when I watched the careful skinning and stretching. He had to peel the fur away from the flesh whole with his skinning knife, even to the tiny toes. Thomas wasn't allowed to skin. One rip ruined a good pelt. Father let Thomas skin our cat that died. Afterwards, Thomas whispered to me that skinning her had made him throw up in the bathroom, quiet so nobody would hear.

I glimpsed a fisher once. Father had said, "Look up, quick," and in the tree I'd seen the flash of darkness, the bouncing of the branch. "Fisher," he'd hissed, and the hiss made me tremble.

With a twig, he dribbled the scent over the bait wired high as he could reach on the leaning tree. The scent was tangy as skunk and fresh as pine needles. One Halloween he smeared it on the doorknob so when the neighbor's kids came begging, they'd get that smell on them to last a while. Father and I laughed and laughed to think of them eating their chocolate.

The steel-wire trap was nailed just below the bait. When set, it made a square for the animal to reach her head through. The trap would snap around the neck.

By the time we reached the farthest-out pond, the sun was gone, the day turned gray. Father left us the matches and told us to warm up while he made a set at the upper end of the "meadow." I called it a bog because of the ice; a beaver bog where dams had backed the water over part of the woods and the trees had died and silvered. Trunks stood straight and silent. Stumps tipped to the air and groped with twisted roots. All my nightmares happened in beaver bogs. I told Thomas they were haunted.

Father saw the snow melted at the top of the beaver house. He knew the beaver were there, breathing. The single beaver he had left alive last year had formed a new colony. He never trapped all the beaver out of this pond because it was so handy to home: just three miles straight out the back door, a new colony almost every year.

Thomas and I watched him stride away up the bog. His tracks were wide apart and straight in a row. Thomas said he wished we'd stayed the hell home.

"We're going to catch some pretty soon," I told him. But I knew he meant we had walked too far and the air was too cold. His buckle boot had a barbwire hole in it that let snow on his sock. His left foot had been frostbitten the winter before. He liked to complain about it.

"I don't care about this," Thomas said. He knew it might

take Father hours to make the pole sets for the beaver. Then three miles to walk home; three and a half with the side trips we had to make for the other fisher traps. We wouldn't be home until dark.

We broke pieces from dead trees. Thomas chopped some low pine limbs at the bog's edge. I peeled birch for a starter.

The ice melted around the log we shared. We took off our boots and rested our sock feet on spruce branches almost in the blaze. Our thawing toes hurt. The smoke rose straight in the air. We ate the cans of sardines Mother had tucked in our coat pockets. We shared the roll of lifesavers and the strong cheese wrapped in brown paper. The snow did not quench our thirst.

Far down the pond we saw Father chopping with his pick: steady, straight-backed, strong. We heard the ring of iron on ice.

The mink traps had been empty when we'd followed the brook in to the pond. One was frozen over so a mink could have walked right on it without harm. Father had smashed the ice without a word. He made Thomas reset the trap, plunging bare hands and arms into the black water. Water seeped out from the fire and turned the snow to gray slush at our feet. Cinders floated. I gathered sticks and watched them flame. I held a brand to the back of Thomas's bent neck to make him jump and knock it away. I threw bits of snow into the fire to hear the sizzle.

Thomas huddled over the warmth. "You didn't have to come, you know," I told him.

"Yes, I did," he said.

"Are you still cold?" I asked.

"Yes!"

I wished I hadn't asked. I wanted him to say, "Course not, damn you."

"He won't be much longer," I said.

"You don't know."

Before Father finished the beaver sets, the flakes had started. They were slow and scattered at first so we hardly noticed, picking up to sting our cheeks and melt on our faces.

I watched the swirling against the sky. I welcomed the snow. Thomas watched it accumulate on his sock through the hole in his boot.

"Should we put the fire out, Father?" We refastened our snowshoes. We pulled hats down and scarves up for the long walk home.

"What's it gonna burn in all this snow, little girl?" He struggled to button his coat around his neck, still sweating from work.

Thomas kicked snow on the fire when Father's back was turned. "Where's it gonna go, Thomas?" I asked.

Father snapped around at us but did not speak. He hurried us. He knew the snow would not stop. The flakes were tiny, fast, wet-falling.

We walked too fast. We walked fast enough to make my side pain and Thomas stagger. I watched the tails of Thomas's snowshoes while the snow fell so heavy I could hardly see anything else. I thought we might go straight home and leave the last two fisher traps for another time, but Father left us sitting in the snow while he took the side path up to the first one.

He'd be right back if the trap was empty. If not, the resetting would take some time. The snow piled on Thomas's shoulders. When Father didn't come back and didn't come back, I stomped my feet, clapped my mittens, and danced in the snow. "Come on, Thomas, dance with me. We'll do a snow dance to be warm." Sometimes in our room Thomas and I danced until we were dizzy. I could barely see him through the snow, but his words were clear and sharp in the silence of woods where even the birds were hiding until the storm passed. "He's taking his sweet time."

"He must have caught something," I said.

"I don't care," Thomas said.

"You should be glad."

"You gonna be a trapper when you grow up, little girl?" he mimicked.

"Shut up," I said. "I don't know why you're so mad just because you're cold. There's worse things than being cold."

I would follow Father's trail. I would walk to meet him. I would help. "He told us to stay here. You better stay here." Thomas grabbed my wrist at the bare part where the mitten didn't meet the cuff. The snow on his mitten stung me.

"I ain't tired," I said. "Are you, Thomas?"

I met Father.

"I told you to wait below," he said. His eyes gleamed.

"What'd you catch?" But I knew.

"A pretty little female, Elizabeth. Peek in the pack." He knelt. Female fisher had the finest fur and brought the best money.

She rested in his basket on top of his traps and ax and scent pouch. I pulled her out and rubbed her back against my face. The fur tickled.

"Can I carry her?"

"Don't drop her or drag her. I don't want no fur rubbed off."

I pulled off my mitten and touched her with my bare hand. The body moved with my pressing, the flesh still soft. Carrying her in my arms, I felt as if I had tamed a wild, living animal.

The snow piled on our snowshoes till we had to kick and push it off. Thomas and I strayed from the trail and tripped on invisible rocks and bushes. Father set too steady a pace. We followed, though, and did not fall far behind because he said not to.

Thomas breathed loud enough for me to hear even at rest. While Father went to tend the final trap, Thomas and I sat close together under a spruce. Father disappeared in darkness. Night had come early with the storm. The low branches kept the snow from striking us directly. I could smell the spruce needles. The snow bent the branches to the ground.

The fisher lay stretched across my lap, her tail in the snow, her head on Thomas's knee.

"He's not coming back," Thomas said through his scarf. "He's going to leave us here and tell Ma we got lost."

"He might leave you the way you act," I said. "But he wouldn't leave me."

Thomas cried, I think, though I really couldn't see.

"You talk foolish, Thomas. You don't talk like my brother."

"I'm cold," he said.

"Just because you're cold . . ."

"He don't care about us, you know," said Thomas.

"We'll be home pretty soon. You'll thaw."

"He don't!"

"How do you know?"

"That's just the way he is," Thomas said. "He does just what he wants. He don't care about nobody."

I knew lots Father cared about. He cared about Mother because she was his wife. He cared about us because we were his kids. He cared about animals and outwitting them.

I held the fisher's face to mine and rubbed the length of her across my lips. She was warm and quiet. I imagined her my pet. If she'd been alive though, she'd have been clawing and biting and fighting me. I loved her dead.

"Your mouth flaps too much," I said, the way Father would have said it.

"If we freeze up, he'll be in trouble."

"Why'd he be in trouble 'cause you were so stupid to freeze

yourself? Why'd you want to get your own father in trouble? You're crazy."

"I hate you," he said, and meant it.

I hugged the dead fisher. I stared out through the close spruce. My eyes strained to follow the tiny flakes that bent the thick branches. I would watch for Father, and he would come. Snow could not stop him.

Saturday Night at the Hi-View Drive-In

If you put too much syrup in the bubbler, the cola will come out as thick and bitter as coffee that has set too long. If you put in too little, it'll be thin, and customers will accuse you of watering it down. So I leave the mixing of cola to Paulie, the snack-bar manager. I don't want to hear about it if it turns out wrong. Same reason I pin my name under the collar of my blouse—the "Judy" hidden, the "Burley" sticking out part way; I don't want to hear about it. I figure Paulie gets paid to manage, let him. Alphonse is Paulie's boss. Al works days for the state crew; nights he runs the drive-in, so he pulls in two salaries all summer long. Winters he puts in a lot of overtime during snowstorms. All in all, he makes good money. He's killing himself, of course. He doesn't sleep. I don't think he sleeps more than three or four hours a night all summer. Al's a young guy—not much older than me really, though he seems older because he's been working a long time. Also, he looks old. Four hours of sleep a night will do that—make your eyes tired, cave your cheeks in, thin your hair. Well, maybe the thin hair he inherited from his father.

Al's saving up to buy a camping area. He believes in ten years there'll be as many tourists around in the summer for camping, hiking, and swimming as come winters to ski. He says they'll be swimming in the river! The river has been cleaned up. No more toilet paper in the mud; just bloodsuckers sticking to your feet when you accidentally touch bottom.

My winter job is behind the counter at "Bradley Mountain—the Pleasure Place." We call it the P.P. More skiers come every winter. Last year they began to complain about the lines, which is a real good sign. If I had to guess, I'd say there were more tourists around this summer than before. I think the camping area is a good idea. I think Al knows what he's doing.

Paulie asked Al once why he wasn't married. Paulie's married with three kids under six. They all have round faces just like Paulie, though theirs aren't as red. They'll get redder as they grow up—like Paulie. High blood pressure, I think. The boys have crew cuts like their father. The little girl looks like somebody put a bowl on her head and cut around it. Paulie thinks the world of her, but he treats his wife like dirt. She probably doesn't think so, but I do. I don't think he beats her, but he makes her stay home with the kids—gives her $25 a week for groceries, tells her if there's any left over she can spend it on herself. Generous, huh?

She had a chance to work at the drive-in. In fact, she could've had my job, but Paulie said he saw enough of her at home. He said that to her face. If I were married and wanted to work, I guess I'd work no matter what my husband said.

Anyway, one night when the three of us were cleaning up— Paulie washing dishes, Al wiping counters, and me sweeping—Paulie asked Al why he wasn't married. I just kept on sweeping. I thought Al might be embarrassed to talk about not being married in front of me. I was curious, though. Al's a good guy with ambition.

Al said he wasn't married because he worked too hard for his money. He'd seen too many guys get married and a year or two later end up divorced—with nothing. The wives got the house, the car, the upright freezer, whatever there was. "They don't care if a guy's been working two jobs since he was sixteen so he could own his own house and put a few decent things in it. And it doesn't seem to matter if you've been married two months or twenty years. They want it; they get it," he said. "I'm not stupid enough to be taken to the cleaners by a woman."

I felt bad for him when he said that. He's a lonely man.

Tonight I have to work the glass box. Taking tickets is my least favorite job, especially on X-rated nights, and that's when I usually get stuck with it because that's when the high-school kids—the part-timers—have to stay in the snack bar. It's the law: nobody under eighteen allowed outside during an X. They're allowed to serve popcorn and listen if they want (there's a speaker behind the counter), but God forbid they should be outside where they might take a peek. Of course, they do watch. Business gets slow and the boys sidle out the side door to stand in the shadows near the men's room. They take it all in. Sometimes the cop will come up and stand right next to them. He doesn't care. He's watching, too. They're all watching.

And here I sit, just about the only female in the place, on a bar stool in a glass box. The light's so strong inside the box that as soon as it gets dark I can't see anything except my own reflection on three sides. My hair starts out smooth and pulled back in a barrette. Then the booth heats up, I begin to sweat, the hair strings around my face, sticks across my forehead. I look like hell but I can't comb it—not sitting there all lit up with cars backed end-to-end all the way to the highway. They can see me, but I can't see them. That's the way of it, since most of them don't come out of the woodwork until after dark. They don't care about catching the beginning of the movie; they just want to be sure nobody driving by sees them waiting to get in. It's like standing in line at the rest room; you don't mind doing it if you have to, but you don't want an audience.

Some leave their headlights on while they wait. Beyond my reflection I can see eight or ten sets of headlights, smaller and smaller down the line. When customers pull up, the booth lights hit them and they draw back—like clams when you poke them with a fork to see if they're alive. They draw back just a little as if the light hurts. Then the hand comes out with the money. I reach through the half-moon window and replace the bills with tickets and change. They drive on.

We need the lights so I can count how many in each car. Usually on X nights, the counting is easy. A man alone—dollar seventy-five; a man and a woman huddling, the woman's face upturned on the man's shoulder as if to prove she isn't embarrassed, or turned away as if she sees something real fascinating out the side window (like a spruce tree or cat's eyes)—three-fifty.

As darkness comes on strong, my hands stiffen with money dirt and the windows turn to mirrors. I can see every blemish on my face, but mostly I notice my double chin, pale and soft, which I hate and can't seem to get rid of no matter how much I weigh. If I lost twenty pounds, the chin would still plague me. I should lose fifteen. I can tell by the way my mother looks at me when I take second helpings at Sunday dinner. She expects me home Sundays and I usually go.

I have gained weight since I moved out. The trouble with cooking for yourself is that you cook just what you like, so you eat too much. One of these days I'll start cooking food I don't like—fish sticks, liver, turkey tetrazzini.

Without the double chin, I wouldn't look half bad. Even now, when I smile, the chin stretches out of sight; my nose is straight enough, my eyes big. One ear is bigger than the other, but you can't tell under my hair. Sometimes I believe if I combed my hair just right and could hold a smile for six or eight hours straight, I could maybe attract a decent man— someone more decent than that creep Mark Ham with his curly red hair and sideburns, so full of himself he wouldn't notice another person half-dead, bleeding or convulsing or cry-ing, across the room.

He thinks he broke up with me and I let him think so be-cause, basically, I am a kind person who'd just as soon not hurt anyone's feelings, though I know Mark would have trouble ima-gining—even if I told him so—that a girl like me, double chin and all, could get sick of him, could become repulsed at the thought of his slimy hand holding hers, his slimy arm around her shoulders. Slimy freckled hand, slimy freckled arm. The man has freckles all over—as far as I know. I mean I never saw all of him, although once at Hampton Beach he squeezed himself into a pair of those black, skimpy swim trunks like the Canadians wear. We sat in the sun for about six hours. He burned all over. He pulled his knees up to his chin and, with his mirror shades in place, watched the girls bounce by. To me he looked like a red squash curled up in the sand, the freckles a brown blight all over. So there I sat in my one-piece with the ruffled skirt that hides unsightly bulges while he ogled other girls.

Why he asked me out in the first place is a mystery. In the city shopping, I met him on the street. Pleased to see someone from home, I smiled a big smile and talked to him like he was a long-lost pal: What are you up to? Do you have a job? Have you seen so-and-so? That kind of friendly talk. I forgot myself; I'm supposed to be shy. In second grade I heard someone de-scribe me as shy, and I figured, why not? I started acting shy and kept it up. In high school, if there'd been a yearbook page for "Most Shy," they'd have put my picture in. Shy is a good safe way to be, though it does wear on a person after a while because of all the things you have to pretend you're too shy to do.

Anyway, the next night Mark called and asked me out. I couldn't believe it. Maybe I did so much smiling that day on the street, he hadn't noticed my chin. Maybe he thought I was pretty. Maybe he thought I was nice. Maybe he was just hard up. I don't know. In high school he went out with pretty girls like Sheri Pritchard, cheerleader. Maybe he was sick of her type. I don't know.

One thing, I don't smile at all while selling tickets from the glass box because somebody might get the wrong idea.

The trouble with Mark is . . . well, his name for one. I couldn't seem to pronounce it the way he wanted me to.

"My name is not Mac," he'd say. "It's Ma-er-k." He pronounced the first sound "Ma" like what I call my mother. He growled the second and choked on the third.

"I know," I'd say. "Mark."

"Not Mac."

"I didn't say Mac; I said Marrrk."

Where he learned to pronounce *r*'s in the middle of words is beyond me, but I just can't seem to get the hang of it. Finally he told me to call him Baby. "Forget it," I said, and ended up calling him nothing at all. He called me Baby once; I told him to cut it out. "I'm not your baby. I'm not a baby," I said. "I like to be called by my name." He looked shocked. Maybe he thought I had no opinion about what anybody called me. Maybe he thought I ought to be happy to be called anything at all.

Same thing, when we rode in his truck he always wanted me right next to him so he could slide his arm around me. It was not a comfortable way to travel, particularly with the floor shift between my legs, but he insisted.

The other trouble with Mark—the main trouble with Mark —was that's as far as it went—the hand holding, snuggling in the truck, kissing on Main Street. One night he grabbed me in front of Laverdiere's and kissed me like we were in a movie (PG, not X). He kissed me for a long time while running his hands up and down my back. I thought I was in heaven. I hoped nobody I knew was watching.

But when we were alone, he lost interest. Not that I wanted to be mauled or anything, but I wouldn't have minded some PG hugs and kisses, some sweet whispers, a wrestling hold or two.

After a few months I began to wonder what was wrong with me. I was sure he'd done more with Sheri Pritchard than sit on the couch and watch TV. At first I thought he was holding off because of some notion that, being shy, I would be embarrassed to be loved. Eventually though, I began to feel there was something so ugly about me inside or out or both that he couldn't force himself to get close.

So I started not answering the phone when I knew it was him. I was sassy and sarcastic when we met. Besides telling him not to call me Baby, I complained about the vertical hold on the TV. I complained about the radio stations he tuned in and the floor shift between my legs. Once I even told him his aftershave turned my stomach, which it did. After a few weeks of that treatment, he said, "Judy, you've changed. I don't think I want to go out with you anymore."

I replied sweetly, "I don't know what you mean, Mark. But if that's how you feel, then I guess that's how it's got to be."

The trouble is I broke up with Mark nearly a year ago, and nobody decent has asked me out since. Sometimes I wonder if I should have been more patient. Sometimes I wonder if I'll ever get another chance.

Behind me, make-believe lovers slurp and groan. The music dies down, making the sounds of the lovers more distinct. Of course I'm curious. Of course I want to turn around for a peek. My neck aches from wanting to turn around for a peek. I mean, I know what's going on, but I'm curious to see for myself. Sounds like they ate something bad at supper—some spoiled tetrazzini, maybe. They slurp it up—then, when it hits the stomach, the groaning starts. Of course I know that's not what's going on, but I have to entertain myself somehow sitting here all lit up and alone in the ticket booth. Even when they scream, I don't look back. I never look at the screen when I'm in the glass box.

Five minutes before intermission, Al will be down to take over so I can work the snack bar. Maybe he'll come down early so we can chat a while. I like visiting with Al, though our chats are never what you'd call chatty. He'll say something kind of sarcastic like: "Big turnout tonight. I guess the word's out." Which might not be sarcastic except for the way he twists his face when he says it, except for the fact that I know he doesn't think much of the movies he shows. For one thing, he could be arrested at any time. Whenever a new movie comes in, the town sends a contingent—chief of police, a selectman or two, sometimes even the county sheriff—to decide whether or not it's pornography. Usually they all arrive together in an official vehicle with writing on the door, bubble lights, and a floppy radio antenna. How they decide about pornography, I don't know. Maybe they sit in there voting. "All those who think this is filth, signal with a 'Yea.' All those who think it's just good fun?"

They haven't closed us down yet; Al hasn't had to go to jail. Though I don't suppose jail would bother him much. He's the kind of guy who takes things in stride, though I know he'd be upset about missing work if they kept him locked up too long. He doesn't like to miss work.

"Yup," I'll say to Al, "looks like they're coming out of the hills for this one. I've sold . . . ," and I'll say how many tickets I've sold to make him feel good. Instead of being paid by the hour like the rest of us, he gets a percentage.

"Yup," he'll say, "the word's out."

Neither of us is a fast talker. Maybe that's why I feel comfortable talking to him. I don't feel like he's analyzing everything I say or counting my r's. When he shows up, I can leave the glass box and move to the snack bar where I'll stuff lukewarm meatballs into submarine rolls. I'd much rather do that than take tickets, even though the sauce dribbles down my fingers and stains my cuffs, even though some people give me the cold stare like I should get my fingers off their meatballs. "My hands are clean," I feel like telling them, "probably cleaner than yours." Al's strict about clean hands in the snack bar. He keeps a can of Boraxo on the counter by the sink; the sign says "Use me." When customers give me the cold stare, I give them the same right back. If you act shy when you're waiting on people, they'll begin to make demands: "A little fuller," they'll say, wanting four meatballs when I'm supposed to put in just three. "More butter," they'll say, when I'm supposed to squirt just once on a small order of popcorn and twice on a large. Not that Al would say anything. He's never spoken a harsh word to me, not even when I came out seven dollars short at the ticket booth. Paulie's the one who makes the rules about how many meatballs and squirts are allowed. And Paulie has a temper I don't care to stir up. So when a customer demands more butter, I put it on quick and hope Paulie doesn't notice.

Still, I'd rather work in the snack bar than the glass box. Two hours in the box and I begin to lose my breath. Tonight, as usual, I've forgotten my watch and the clock's broken, so I try to read the upside-down watches on the hands that slide in and out of my half-moon window. Frayed shirt cuffs, hairy arms, tattoos, bug bites, warts, Band Aids, sores, oil stains, freckles—a hand covered with freckles. I recognize those freckles.

"Mark?" the name slides out before I can catch it. I forgot to pronounce the r.

I haven't seen him for a long time—months. Not face to

face like this, nose to nose, since he's in the pickup, sitting up there pretty high. I've seen him in the distance a couple of times, on the street with time enough to cross to the other side and avoid him. Not that I need to avoid him; it's just that I have nothing to say. Here, with lovers behind me fifty feet high, wrestling across the night sky, and the man who might have been my lover in front of me with the booth lights in his face, I find myself with less to say than usual. Yet I feel like I should say something.

Under the lights every freckle shows. His eyes are pink, un-blinking as he leans out the truck window. I feel like I'm in a who-will-blink-first contest. I quit. I blink.

"One," he says.

"Dollar seventy-five," I say, taking the five and handing back a quarter and three bills. He's wearing his class ring, a sapphire in a white gold setting. It is a big fat ring. Once he offered it to me—to wear, you know how high-school girls do, with yarn wound around a hundred times for fit, or on chains around their necks. I told him that was kid stuff, which it is.

"How long you been working here, Judy?" he asks. He still hasn't blinked. Maybe his eyes are glued open.

"Since spring," I say. Then, because there are no cars wait-ing and because he's staring as though he expects more, I add, "What about you? Still at the tech school?"

"Part-time," he says, pronouncing the r carefully, spitting out both t's. I guess they teach you how to pronounce t's at the tech. He stares beyond me, at the screen. He's pretending to be talking to me, but staring at nude people on the screen. (I assume they're nude from the look in his eyes.) He shuts his engine off like I've got nothing better to do than watch him watch the movie, than wait for him to decide whether he has something else to say to me. He's sitting there like I invited him.

I never liked his attitude. I only went out with him because
... because I wanted to see what it was like to go out with
someone. Sad but true. He has no right to sit there in his big
black truck staring at me and through me and beyond me with
his little pink eyes. Men alone who pull up to this booth keep
their eyes down. They don't look at me, and I don't look at
them.

Mark told me once that he's the type of guy other guys like
to pick fights with. He claimed something about the way he
walks or carries himself seems to antagonize the guys who so-
cialize on street corners—young guys who quit school and
work the graveyard shift if they work at all, guys with bottles in
the pockets of their leather jackets. He seemed proud of his
ability to cause trouble. "I can talk my way out of a fight," he
said. "If I want to. Most of the time I just keep walking by. I
just ignore them. They don't really want to fight me; they just
think they do."

He's acting like he wants to fight me. My father says never
stare a mean dog in the eyes. He says that makes the dog want
to defend his territory. I feel like defending something. I feel
like he's mocking me. The glass separates us though, so I
couldn't punch his face even if I wanted to—which I do, sort
of. It's a strange feeling. I've never wanted to punch a face
before.

He seems proud to be alone at an X-rated movie where he
can sit in his comfy cab in the dark and think whatever obscene
thoughts he wants to think, do just as he likes. He seems
pleased that Judy Burley knows he'll be thinking obscene
thoughts and doing just as he likes, alone. On the other hand,
maybe he's not so proud, maybe he feels found out, maybe he's
embarrassed to be twenty years old and all alone at the Hi-View
on Saturday night. Maybe he's bluffing. Maybe he's been one
big, freckled bluff all along.

Then Al's behind me in the booth. I jump a little because I didn't hear him open the door. The whoosh of fresh air feels good. Close quarters though; we can't help but brush shoulders as I move off the stool and he moves on.

"Paulie needs you at the snack bar, Judy," he says. Al hardly ever calls me by my name. I like the way he says my name, soft and slurred. No doubt he's wondering why this joker is parked in front of the ticket booth. No doubt he's going to say something about it if the joker doesn't move along soon. I can hardly wait.

Mark tries the stare treatment on Al, but Al won't put up with it. He laughs a kind of clearing-your-throat laugh and says, "What's the matter, buddy? Judy give you the wrong change, or is your truck broke?"

Mark doesn't answer. He turns the key fast, lets the clutch out too quick so the truck lurches forward. Al and I are silent for a minute or two as we watch the truck lights travel down one row, up another. Mark's being choosy about where to park it. Somebody toots; they don't like his lights and noise this far into the movie.

"What a jerk," Al says.

"He is a jerk," I say. If Al says he's a jerk, then he must be one; he must have been one all along. I give Al a big smile. I feel my double chin stretch out of sight. I wonder if he knows what I'm smiling about.

"I can't believe I ever went out with him," I say, to let Al know I'm the kind of girl men sometimes ask out; it seems important to let him know that if someone were to ask me out I probably wouldn't hurt his feelings by saying no, even if the guy were a jerk, which, of course, Al isn't. "Thanks for getting rid of him," I say. "He can't take a hint."

"No problem," Al says.

I run between the parked cars from row to row toward the

lighted snack bar. I'm careful not to look inside any cars. I don't want to see what's going on. I don't want to know. I concentrate on rear bumpers, license plates, and speaker posts.

Paulie's behind the counter looking harried, as usual. His white apron is buttered up and his forearms are orange with meatball juice. The coffee machine's broken, so he's been mixing instant in Styrofoam cups on the spot. The counter is brown and sticky with coffee. Sweat has streaked his face and plastered his collar to his neck. The collar's in love with him, clinging when he pulls at it with a thick, orange finger. Even with the top button open, this shirt, like all his shirts, seems too snug at the neck, riding up, riding down with his Adam's apple. He won't unbutton a second button. I don't know why: maybe he's got a tattoo on his collarbone or something; maybe he's bald-chested. Paulie's all right to work with as long as you don't make him mad, but he treats his wife like dirt. Maybe buying shirts a size too small is her way of paying him back.

I think of Al down in the glass box, waiting for those last few customers to straggle in—dollar seventy-five, three-fifty, dollar seventy-five—his percentage night after night adding up to a gold mine of a campground on the side of the mountain: electric hookups, running water, one-holers nice and clean, firewood for sale by the bundle or cut-your-own deadwood. His own place, his own work, no more moonlighting. The man will be able to sleep eight hours a night in his own little cabin in the woods. He'll have time to rest, time to think about something besides work, time to think about the help he needs and how lonely he is—time to be lonely and do something about it.

I wonder how long it'll take him to realize that I, Judy Burley, am not the kind of woman who would ever hurt a man like him, not the kind of woman who would ever take a good, kind, hard-working man like him to the cleaners.

﷽ Eva on the Beach

Eva anonymous on the beach under her big hat. Sun penetrates the weave, dappling the world, dappling the fisherman, just yards away, thick through the neck and jowls, a mole almost an inch across, prominent on his red-veined cheek. She thinks of tropical fish and color camouflage, the appearance of an eye where an eye might be, but isn't.

The fisherman watches his taut line, his pole propped on a forked stick. He sits on his beer cooler, smokes a cigarette, ignores Eva. Her daughter Louanne and Louanne's friend Shenita race to the water shrieking, tumbling under, exciting the dog, who whines and strains the leash. Their wake slaps the shore. Her son Patrick wades in. Water darkens the hem of his trunks. His friend Roy belly-flops, soaking him.

It is one of those shocking hot afternoons in May, before winter blood has thinned to tolerate spring heat. The dog plows toward the water. Eva braces herself, steps aside when he tries to wind her ankles. He is a heavy dog—part Basset, a close-to-the-ground dog, a stubborn boy. He claws the sand at the water's edge. He was her husband's dog. "Take the dog," she said, when he left. When he left her, and her children. But he left the dog behind, too. "Get angry," her friends tell her. "He betrayed you."

"I am angry," she tells them. But she's not. She's bewildered. Apparently, in their marriage, her reality had not been his. "I want to make this as easy on you and the kids as I can," he said, leaving.

"Stop it," she tells the dog. "Stop it or I'll put you in the car—I mean it." He growls. "Don't you dare growl at me." She draws a deep breath and releases it in a sigh so deep it hurts her throat. She ties the dog to the picnic table. Sits in her beach chair, smoothes her newspaper over her knees. The late-afternoon sun warms the curl of shore.

Louanne yells, "Can we go out to the sandbar?"

"No," Eva says.

"We always play on the sandbar," Patrick yells. He doesn't say, Daddy would let us.

"Just be careful," she says, watching the braiding of the water. She follows with sore eyes until all three have found the relative safety of the shallow out deep. Then she lets her eyelids fall, watches the shooting stars, and wills herself to stop thinking, to just be. Eva on the beach. Eva by healing water. Healing sun.

The voices fade. The fisherman coughs. The dog sleeps. The breeze rattles her newspaper and rustles the leaves of the oak tree that marks the edge of the fishing area. She opens her eyes. Red and white bobbers dangle from the limbs like Christmas ornaments. The fisherman turns hard eyes on Eva, silver glints in wells of puffed flesh. The mole is like a third eye, blank and unblinking.

Thirty feet out, in the shallow over the sandbar, Shenita straddles Louanne's shoulders; Patrick clings to Roy's with blue knees. They push each other above and below. Shenita screams when Louanne loses her balance and ducks under. *They'll hurt themselves*, Eva thinks. "We didn't mean to," they'll say. "I don't want to hurt anybody," her husband said.

As the children play, their position shifts, gradually toward the fisherman and forbidden territory, where the sand turns to muck and lost hooks booby-trap the sediment.

The fisherman throws down the stub of his cigarette. It lands beside his water-darkened boot, a finger of smoke curling up. He exhales loudly, mumbles an angry something, staccato under his breath. *Is he talking to me?* Eva wonders. The dog lifts its head.

Another mother might yell, "Calm down, you kids. Stay away from the fisherman. And be careful." On another day, in another life, Eva might have. But she's lost her voice. Or perhaps it's been taken from her. *We have as much right to this beach as the fisherman*, she thinks.

And if a child gets a foot in the face or an elbow in the collarbone or a hook in the toe, she will touch the hurt spot, apply antiseptic, find a Band Aid, and that is all, all she will do, all she can do. Who could do more?

The fisherman is reeling in. His line slices the water. There is no fish on his hook. The line moves too easily for that, the tip of the pole vibrating but not bending.

Now the kids are playing shark. Roy is the shark. The others scream and evade as he dives down, then pops up in unexpected places. They churn the water. Another mother might warn, "Quiet down, you kids." Or, "Get back to your own side." On another day, in another life, Eva might have. Instead, she pulls her hat low over her face; the weave breaks the light into diamonds. When she closes her eyes, she can still see them.

The fisherman pinches the leader, cuts it with his jackknife. The hook, still threaded with salmon eggs, falls to the ground beside his boot and the smoldering cigarette. From the tackle box, he pulls a silvery lure dangling three large hooks. He does not look at Eva. He knots the lure, then, with a turn of the reel, snugs it to the tip of the pole. Swings. Lets fly.

The lure arcs, drawing the line behind it. It sails past Louanne's right ear. It smacks the water in the midst of the children. The lure is underwater now, sinking. The children, silenced, stand very still. Patrick bends to see where the lure has gone, but he can't get his eye on it—moving water, broken reflections. Water to her chest, Shenita raises her arms in surrender.

Eva rises from her chair even as the fisherman is maneuvering the lure out from among the children. The dog is also on its feet, on Eva's feet, toenails digging in. The newspaper has fallen, the folds opening, breeze separating the pages. A page blows into the water where it begins to soak and sink. Eva pushes the dog out of her way, sick at her stomach.

She sees the shadow of the lure twisting toward shore. It drags the muck in the shallows. The fisherman raises his pole; the lure drips weed and hooks. Eva has moved, swiftly and silently, to within an arm's length of the fisherman, eye to eye; fingering sun on the back of her neck, sweat in her clenched hands, the hard curve of the ground under her feet.

He shrugs. "What? You got a problem?"

He could have put out a child's eye with that cast. He could have punctured an artery.

He swings his arm up and straight back as though to cast again. She steps in front of him, tasting blood. She doesn't remember biting her cheek. She places her body between him and the water and the children. She raises her arm, spreads her fingers as though she'll block his swing by grabbing his wrist, thick, pale on the underside. For a moment, she thinks he's going to bring the rod down on her head.

He squints. Two eyes squinting, but the mole still round and smooth, mocking her.

"The wind took it," he says. "I wasn't no more aiming for them kids than . . . Christ, lady. Good Christ, what is your problem?" Then he laughs in his throat and Eva remembers anger. She raises both hands to form a mime's wall between them and leans into it, so close she can see the flattened body of a mosquito, an asterisk on the vein in his neck. His smoky breath heats her face. When her eyes blur, she blinks the soft scales away and they fall on her cheeks like tears. She looks him right in the mole and speaks. The soft growl is the one a survivor heeds. "You are a liar," she begins.

⚏ Bonfire

That Joey Frye was dead didn't surprise me. I'd been anticipating his death for a long time. I dreamed of it. My mother enclosed his obituary in her letter. After a few wheedling sentences about my relationship with the man she thinks I'm going to marry, she explained that Joey died of heart failure brought on by chemotherapy for leukemia. His third wife was planning to sue the hospital, though she didn't need the money. Joey had life insurance.

In the album, I find the photograph of my brother David and Joey and me. Three little kids walking toward the camera. Joey looking off, distracted. Those big ears, that blond fuzz of hair—wiffle cut, wiffle boy. David and I seem to walk with the same stride, the same inquisitive tilts to our heads, mouths open as though we're making the same sassy comment.

Joey, tough boy from the toughest family on our road, dead at thirty-three and his third wife—slut that she must have been to have married the likes of him—a rich widow. "He has a tough row to hoe," my mother once said in his defense. I wonder if she remembers feeling sorry for Joey Frye, whose death does not sadden me, but reminds me, hurtles me back twenty-one years to the night of the bonfire.

.   .   .

Snow still on the ground, but not deep enough to bother, we took the short cut across the field—mother, father, sister,

brother—everybody looking forward to the bonfire. Oven mitts
on both hands, my mother carried hot tuna casserole in a covered dish. My father pushed a wheelbarrow overflowing with
the remains of the willow that split during the storm. He'd already made a few trips back and forth with brush from the
woodlot he was clearing for our park. When the woods were
cleared, he said, he'd build a seesaw, swing, tree house, put up
a basketball hoop—the works. For David and me, imagining
the park was almost as good as having it. We'd already flagged
the tree-house tree.

When Ma and Dad weren't looking, I pushed David's hat
over his eyes, snappy black eyes, like my mother's, like mine.
He pretended to fall, knocked me down. We wrestled in what
was left of the snow. My mother said, "Jessie, David, is that
necessary?" But she didn't have time to be mad, because my
father was pretending to run over her with the wheelbarrow.
She danced out of the way, casserole and all. David grabbed
my hat and ran off with it. "Brat," I shouted after him. "Eat
snow," he shouted back. "Drop dead," I said.

It was a beautiful night for a bonfire. Winter was evaporating
in the ground fog of melting snow. Cold enough to see your
breath with every syllable, but not so cold you couldn't stand
it for the long periods of standing around and what my father
called "heavy-looking-on" that tending a bonfire requires. An
armload of brush added to the pile, a rotted trunk thrown on
to tamp it, a poke here and there.

We were impressed when we saw the mountain of brush
behind Uncle Al's house—we called many of the adults in the
neighborhood Aunt and Uncle, though they were no blood relation. I snagged my hat out of David's hand while he was busy
being impressed. We'd had bonfires before, but never this big.
It had been a hard winter, lots of snow, wind, tree-snapping ice
storms. The flames would light the world. David said: "It's

gonna be a volcano!" We watched as Uncle Al lit the news-
papers. The fire spread to cardboard boxes laced with gasoline,
then came the big roar and the wood starting to burn and the
flames reaching up. Fire in the sky.

Joey was there. I wasn't happy to see him. I remembered
what he'd done to the worm in science class earlier in the week
when Mrs. Z told him to poke it gently and watch it move. He
waited until he knew I was looking, then skewered it with his
sharp pencil. "That's a detention," Mrs. Z. said. But detentions
didn't bother Joey.

When he spotted David in the firelight, he punched his arm
and grabbed him by the coat. David grinned.

My mother and the Aunts often talked over coffee about
how to raise kids. They agreed that good mothers stayed home.
If Joey's mother had been home, instead of working, they said,
he wouldn't have stolen money from the jar the Halliseys, stu-
pidly, displayed in their picture window. If Joey's mother had
been around, he wouldn't have set the fire that burned all the
grass in the hollow and almost jumped the stream to the box
factory. If Joey's mother had been around, he wouldn't have
killed that cat. Joey was accused of these crimes and others. He
denied everything.

"Joey's a good boy," his mother would say. "If he says he
didn't do it, he didn't do it." His father said, "If I find out different, by God, I'll thrash him myself." His father had flittering
eyes and acne scars that made his face hard to look at. I
wondered if he scared Joey as much as he scared David
and me. When Old Man Frye was around, we all tried to
fade away.

Someone offered the skeleton of a Christmas tree to the fire.
It crackled. Sparks flew straight up like Fourth of July, then
showered us. "Get back," a gruff Uncle warned. "You kids get
away from that fire right now."

Joey grabbed David and they ran into the darkness, whooping. I smothered a spark that landed on my friend Kathy's hood—a rabbit fur hat with the pompoms, a soft hood that framed her long pale face. Flames danced over the curve of her wire-rim glasses.

Uncle Al threw a plank on. Sparks, ash, embers shot out. Kathy and I jumped back. "We're on fire," she said.

"David was right," I said. "The volcano's erupting."

Our faces grew hot from the flames, reflecting red, hot and dry, the air cold, growing colder. Our clothes, damp from brush and leaves we helped move, were steaming. We roasted hot dogs on long sticks, charred on the outside, cold in the middle. Ashes stuck to our teeth.

We watched Uncle Al—glug, glug, the pale fold of skin at his throat moving as he drank deeply from a wineskin, then passed it on. The men were laughing, their faces flushed from the alcohol, their shadows jumping. The Aunts were drinking cocktails down at the house in the lighted sun-room. I could see them through the floor-to-ceiling glass—smiling women in bright dresses, arranging and rearranging food on the long, folding table. I could see the Aunts' mouths moving, flashes of teeth between lips remarkable for their redness and mobility. I saw them talking, talking, but heard the Uncles' low voices and rumbling laughter—an eerie ventriloquism. My mother and the Aunts dancing behind glass, my father and the men talking, the fire snapping, Kathy warm and close by, my brother playing night stalker somewhere in the dark. I expected him to tackle me any moment, to leap out of the darkness. I wouldn't be scared, though. I'd be laughing.

All was in order. The last perfect moment.

Then came the screech. The screech that lasted too long. The sound from across the field of wheels locking, tires melting over tar. It was a terrifying sound that lasted too long to be just a teenager from the trailer park peeling rubber—too long to be a stranger driving too fast, surprised by the hairpin curve. Too long.

The men were silenced. All human activity stopped and the sounds of the fire filled us—hiss and crackle and flame and the searing wind.

Then the men started running toward the road—racing out across the field, finding the shortest route toward the lights of a car off the road and tipped at a strange angle. The men were running. Kathy and I were running too. The lights were there one moment and gone the next. Suddenly we were running toward darkness.

Kathy and I fell behind. We fell two or three times on the uneven ground which rose to trip us. She pulled me up. I pulled her up. We could hear the anxious voices of our mothers far away. They'd opened the sliding glass doors; some had ventured into the slushy yard, calling out, "What's wrong? What's happened?"

By the time Kathy and I reached the road, Uncles were all over it. Their dark forms moved in another kind of dance, this one slow, graceless, confused. Men heavy with knowledge, clumsy with shock.

A car came around the corner too fast. Men stepped out to stop it. "Keep your headlights on," they said. "Headlights! We can't see what the hell we're doing."

Kathy and I scrunched behind a snow bank, knowing if seen we'd be sent away. There was a car in the ditch, the hulk of a car, the gleam of glass and chrome. The driver was climbing out. The ceiling light came on when the door opened and stayed on. I could see the curve of the seats, the tilted dash, a tissue box in the back window.

Uncles embraced the driver as he staggered toward them. They fell with him to the ground where, when they moved away, I could see that he'd pulled his knees to his face and locked his arms over his head.

Then someone was separating himself from another cluster of Uncles, lurching toward the driver: "I'll kill you. You bastard. I'll kill you."

I didn't recognize the voice, though of course it was my father's. Uncles wrapped themselves around him. "The ambulance is coming," they said.

I heard the siren in the distance. I heard Kathy sniffling. "Shhhh," I said, angry. "They'll hear you. Stop it." Her sniffling was so loud I thought my head would burst with it. "Shut up," I said. The others seemed far away. Small figures moving now in the blue light from the police cars; now in red light from the ambulance. Small Uncles shrinking before my eyes. I saw my father clutch his stomach as though in pain. He was shrinking faster than the others. Back at the house, I didn't know it but my mother was shrinking too.

Then I saw Joey on the side of the road, a small dark ball of a boy. I could make out the white of his face, the wiffle cut. Mr. Frye stalked over to him, thin as a black paper cut-out of a man. He yanked Joey to his feet, shook him, dragged him into the road. "That could've been you," he yelled. "That could've been you!"

Joey twisted his face away, but his father put one hand on Joey's shoulder and one on the back of his head, turned him so he had to look.

There was a mound in the middle of the road. I knew it was there. I'd seen it from the first, but pretended not to. I was good at pretending. I still am.

They had covered David with a blanket or a coat, something dark and heavy enough to resist the wind picking up, the wind like frozen fingers squeezing the back of my neck. Away across the field, the wind tore at the bonfire and the flames fought back, bigger and stronger than ever. Fireworks. Fire in the sky.

In the road, the light strobed. Blue lights, red lights, flashing lights, I could hardly see at all—like in a dream when you try to see but you just can't raise your heavy lids. Blind girl. And you can't see the speaker but the voice says, "Once the cut is made, it never stops bleeding."

I don't remember seeing my brother's body uncovered, though I may have. The Uncles knew right away that he was dead, well before the ambulance came, and none of them a doctor.

My recurring dream was, and is, that Joey died, not David. In the dream David smiles because I'm surprised to see him. He says, "Jessie, it wasn't me. It was Joey." In the dream his black eyes snap like embers, and I see the cabin deep in the woods where he's been living all these years and I say, "Why didn't you tell me?"

Days later when Kathy, imitating Aunts, said, "Only the good die young," I felt our friendship begin to end. This I cannot resolve: What were David and Joey doing in that awful wet darkness, in the middle of the road, at night, the ground fog rising? Where did they think they were going?

About a week afterwards came a thunderstorm—a banger in the middle of the night that troubled my sleep. Lightning flashed my dreams through closed eyelids. Before waking, I dreamed of nuclear holocaust. The lightning came into my dreams like the big boom, the flash of blinding light, the mushroom cloud. I dreamed the bomb had fallen and we were all going to die. And I was glad. I was comforted. David had simply gone on ahead. I'd be joining him soon.

But the world did not end. I woke up empty, wanting. I'm still wanting—too much according to the man I could not love. I take no satisfaction in Joey Frye's untimely death. I wish to God I could. "You don't know what you want," said the man I no longer plan to marry. But I do. I want my brother back.

⌗ The White Room

The dead tree, a stump really, was unusual because it had three limbs intact, still sturdy and reaching for the sky. The bark was gone, the wood bleached white and purified by wind, rain, sun; the grain stood distinct, textured. Driftwood on the river bank, high and dry now that the water was down for the summer. Marie enlisted her Uncle Octave to help drag the tree back to the house.

It took a deal of manipulation to get it up the stairs to the second floor. He had to take the door from its hinges and maneuver the limbs just so into the white room where they both pushed hard until it wedged tight ceiling-to-floor, not to be moved again without a crowbar. Once in place, the tree looked as though it had grown there.

Uncle Octave clapped his hands at a job well done. He danced and chanted. There was Abenaki blood in the family—but Marie didn't suppose he was performing an authentic dance: he'd just invented one to make her smile. Octave was the clown among her mother's five brothers—all of whom had come home for her funeral, four of whom had already disappeared again into the world.

The most musically talented of the LaVallee brothers, Octave was a son-and-dance man who played squeeze-box, harmonica, banjo, and, sometimes, guitar. He could also tap-dance, juggle, walk on his hands, touch the tip of his nose with his tongue, and flap his tongue like bird wings.

Marie knew that eventually he too would disappear into the world—leaving her alone in the house when Pepère was away, alone in the dark when Pepère worked the night train or had a Boston layover. But for now, Octave slept in the small room behind the kitchen and Marie slept better knowing he was there: the house was a big one, and—though she had lived in it all her life—there were nooks, stairwells, trapdoors, and shadows that frightened her, but mostly the white room.

"This will be a safe place for animals," she told Octave, having devised big plans: fallen birds nurtured to maturity, cat-wounded chipmunks restored to health, a colony of painted turtles, frogs from the backwater, mice live-trapped and caged out of harm's way, barn spiders in each corner. The tree would be the centerpiece for her menagerie.

When she told her mother how the white room frightened her, Mother said: "Then it is yours."

"I won't sleep in it," Marie said. "I won't sleep in that creepy place." The walls were smooth plaster and the two small windows faced evergreen woods pressed to the north corner of the house.

"Not to sleep in," her mother said. "You have your bedroom for sleeping. This will be a room for play and adventure."

"I don't want it," Marie said.

Mother brought out the sketchbook. "The ceiling will be the sky," she said. "Fair weather clouds"—she traced them with charcoal pencil—"and color." With her palette knife she mixed and spread three distinct blues. "A sky full of color," she said, daubing pink-blue, silver-blue, and lavender.

"And the walls," she said, "how shall we paint your walls? The ocean? The desert? A field of wildflowers."

"Yes, the ocean," Marie agreed. But a calm ocean with mist rising, an ocean so tame a girl could easily spot the black head of a seal. And for the other walls—scenes she knew: the sandbar in the river where the birches hung low; the apple tree when the grass was high and the black-eyed Susans blooming; the shining granite ledge among the hemlock.

Mother sketched each scene. "Use the pastels to suggest the colors," she said. But Marie was afraid she'd ruin the pictures. Though she loved to draw and paint, though she spent many hours alongside her mother working with pencil, pastels, water colors, even oils, Marie's pictures were—to her own eye—never good enough. Her mother's pictures were round, living—inviting a person to step in and find a world.

"All right then," Mother compromised, "you tell me which colors and where." Marie pressed the pastel sticks one at a time into her mother's open, steady hand.

They could not start painting the walls themselves until they had the proper paint, and plenty of it. Pepère agreed to buy the paint for them in Boston when he had to stay the night on layover.

The first week he brought home forest green and pale yellow. The second week it was cherry red and sapphire blue. A quart of each, week after week until the closet floor was cobbled with paint cans. They would start the project as soon as all the paint was assembled. They would start when Mother felt better.

But she only felt worse. Her hands shook. Her eyes sank. She couldn't lift her head from the pillow. Then she died. The brothers whirled in and filled the house. Pepère sat silent in the big chair, surrounded by his noisy sons. He couldn't keep his hands still. Tap, tap on the arm of the chair. Tap, tap. Tap, tap. Marie watched from a silence of her own. All these strangers in the house—Babineau, Arthur, Emery, Louis, and Octave. Soon, only Octave remained.

More than anything, Marie wanted a squirrel for the tree in the white room. A family of red squirrels lived in the stone wall along the garden. The cat had already caught and killed two of them. Marie wanted to capture and tame one—to save it from the cat, which would get them all eventually; he was a hunter, that fellow.

The squirrel would live in the white room and make it the happy place her mother had intended. Marie had found a small turtle and built a box home for it in one corner, but that slow, quiet life had failed to drive the creepy feelings away. A squirrel was called for—lively and mischievous—to cause all manner of havoc: a pet as quick and irreverent as Uncle Octave himself.

Marie lured the squirrels with sunflower seeds. She noted favorite exit holes among the stones and positioned herself, like the cat, in pouncing position. It was a long wait, all one afternoon, while Pepère was away at work—riding the train to somewhere and back—and Octave practiced banjo on the porch. She waited and watched, her legs cramping under her, mosquitoes drilling her flesh, pine odors rising when the sun baked the needles, the clouds moving in the sky.

The first time a squirrel head poked out of the hole, she did not move—but her whole body went on alert and her hands curled in readiness. Next, when the squirrel poked all the way out, Marie grabbed for it and caught fur. Her hand closed around the squirming body and held firm even when the tiny teeth sank deep and the blood came.

She held on and ran for the house yelling, "Open the door, open the door!" Octave held the screen as she whirled through, up the stairs and into the white room, kicking the door shut behind her. Then she shook the squirrel off. He found his legs, zoomed up the tree and stood on the highest limb screaming.

Octave slipped into the room before she could say close the door.

"What the hyde is going on?" he said.

"I caught a squirrel," she said, "for my tree. I told you I wanted a squirrel and a bird and a rabbit and spiders."

He said: "You have blood all over yourself."

Her arm was slick with it, her shirt badly stained, her hand throbbing. The pain made her sit down quick on the floor.

Octave brought a wet rag and washed the blood away. The squirrel had located a window and was clawing the glass. He ran around the room once, testing every corner. He ran over Marie's foot, then back up the tree.

Octave made her drink a glass of water. She watched the squirrel racing back and forth on the limb. Octave smeared her hand with stinging medicine and wrapped it gently. "Hurt like Hades," he said. "Just so it doesn't get infected!"

"I grabbed him and he bit me, but I wouldn't let go," she said. "I figured he could bite me and make me let go and I'd be bitten for nothing; or I could just hold on. So I did."

They sat side by side on the floor. Uncle Octave's legs were not much longer than her own—and he was a grown man, but a small one, the smallest of the brothers, light enough to ride across the field on Babineau's shoulders.

"I think the squirrel will need a cage until it's tamed," she said.

"I can build a cage," Octave said. "I will do that for you."

"Yes," she said. "If I sketch it—will you build it just the way I want it to be?"

"How do you want it to be, Marie?" he teased.

She found the sketchbook in the closet, turned quickly past the sketches her mother had made—the sky, the ocean, the sandbar, the apple tree, the granite ledge—to a blank page near the end. The bandage made it awkward—but not impossible—to hold the charcoal. Her hand hurt, but all the fingers moved.

But before she could draw a line, Octave lifted her hand from the page and placed it on her knee. "Let's see," he said, turning back to the color sketches, examining them one by one.

"Did you draw these, Marie?"

She shook her head. "We were going to paint these pictures on the walls," she said. "Pepère bought the paint and everything."

"Then it should be done," he said. "Definitely."

He laid the sketch of the ocean on the floor in front of them. "Stare at it," he said. "Take it into your heart."

They stared at it together for a long, long time—the grays and blues and whites, the tinges of pink and yellow. She saw how the colors fit together like clasped hands, how they balanced the smooth, black head of the seal.

When Marie raised her head, she saw the picture transposed on the white wall, projected there—huge and in full color.

"I see it," she said. "There, on the wall. Can you?"

"Paint it," he said. "Paint what you see."

"But it's all there," she said. "All that's left is to mix the colors and fill them in where they go. That's too easy," she said. "That's not fair."

"It's your mother's gift," he said. "Accept it."

By first frost, the squirrel was eating from Marie's scarred hand and chattering from her shoulder. Octave had returned to the world, but promised to visit at Christmas. The white room was no longer white. When Marie ran out of walls to paint, she worked on canvas. She painted every day. She painted the life she knew.

Babineau, home to help shingle the barn roof, observed that Marie was even more talented than her mother had been. Pepère nearly struck him when he said that. But deep down Pepère knew—they all knew—that Marie's was a gift which could not be contained.

⌦ The Fisher Cat

I sit alone in the bait shop all night. I don't bother to turn on a light or stoke the stove. I let the fire die to embers, then to stone cold nothing. I want to be cold. I want to feel the cold deep, here in my bait shop among the drive belts, bogie wheels, spark plugs, shiner pails and Swedish Pimples. My father is dead. My mother is dead. And my wife and babies have left me. I could tell this story funny, if I wanted. Poor sap, all alone. Poor stupid Richie, alone in the dark and cold. It'd be funny if it wasn't about me, if I had some idea, any idea, what the hell I'm supposed to do now.

Tomorrow, daylight, the ice fishermen will start in. They'll pound the locked door. They'll give me no peace until I open up—each mother's son of them demanding a dozen shiners, two dozen, three. A lively shiner will lure a pickerel to a man's hook and Luckypine Pond is chuck-full of pickerel, always has been. My shiners are the liveliest around. And the fishermen, knowing this, will not let me be on a fine winter's day with the ice fifteen inches thick on Luckypine Pond—a body of water I know as well as I know myself, having swum it, fished it, even drunk its water boiled when my mother and father and I lived at camp and the well ran dry. Camp's caved in ten years ago, and mother and father gone within weeks of one another—that double loss, that particular hardship coming before I was even a man. They said my mother, having died so hard, came back for my father—and took him quick to spare him agony. Isn't that a hell of a thing to say—a hell of a thing to let a broken-hearted kid overhear?

Anyway, by noon tomorrow, my selling will be done for the day and I'll be free to join the fools on the ice. We'll build a small fire for cooking sausages on sticks. We'll watch for flags and run like hell when one pops up—though more often than not it will be the wind that triggered it. We'll pour muscatel from the gallon jug into paper cups and sip it to warm our bones. When a stranger comes by on his snowmobile and asks what's in the jug, we'll claim—as my father once claimed to a curious Reverend: "It's a special mixture we pour in the holes; keeps 'em from freezing over." Then we'll laugh joke's-on-you laughs to think any fool would believe such a lie.

I'll bring home pickerel for supper. But I'll have to cook them myself. No wife to ream me out for staying away so long when the washing machine backed up and spewed suds all over the kitchen floor. (How was I supposed to know that was going to happen, huh? What does she expect, a mind reader?) No wife to remind me to fillet the fish carefully. No baby girls who might choke on a bone.

I come from a long line of hunters, trappers, and fishermen. Though we must have moved here from somewhere else originally, I know for sure of six generations which have called this town, this land, home. In a way, my bait shop—and the knowledge of the generations that helps me run it—is my inheritance. Gloria doesn't understand that. She doesn't want to understand that.

My grandfather said in his time a man was lucky to earn a dollar working out all day on the state road or in the mica mines, but he could get ten dollars for a fox pelt and that's how the family finally made it through.

My father, at eight years old, was free to wander the village. At ten he had his own gun and spent full days hunting alone.

His mother—the immigrant—might not have approved, but she didn't interfere. They said this of her: The woman never spoke a judgmental word. My mother, once the most beautiful girl in the village, boiled with judgmental words. There was a right way and a right time. My father and I were not good at anticipating these, so she spent her best years setting us straight.

I married a woman like my mother: beautiful, opinionated and sharp in her expression of those opinions. Very sharp. Sharp as the honed blade of a skinning knife, though in the early days when we were falling in love, the sharpness was muted, or it seemed so, because we were careful around one another, careful and kind. We went with each other in high school. (She was two years behind me.) We got married after her graduation, had three little girls right off the bat—bing, bing, bing—so I ended up living among women. For a joke I said I lived in the land of women. Even the dog was female. I wondered what my father would have thought of that.

For five and a half years I pulled wire at the plant to support the family. The money was good but the building held the heat, and I never could take the heat. It was a constant heat—summer and winter, heat from bodies and machinery and too much talk all closed in. It was the kind of heat a man like me could stand for a while but not forever. Pretty soon I could taste the copper all the time. Potatoes tasted copper. Beer tasted copper. My own spit tasted copper.

When the work slowed, they put me on nights with this foreman who had a good word for nobody. A fat, square-headed, moist-lipped pig of a man, Joseph Bottomley—also known as Joe Blow—had delusions of a front-office promotion if he could get the poor saps he supervised to up quota fifteen percent. That meant nights, overtime, weekends. I needed the money. I bowed my head and took his yap. I stood that treatment just as long as I could.

"Gloria," I said, "I'm not cut out to work for other people, especially jerks like Joe Blow. I'm an independent guy. I should be my own boss. It's in my blood."

She said: "If you didn't want to work, why did you marry me? Why did you get me pregnant with these three little babies? Or do you want *me* to go back to work at the restaurant—is that it? You want to stay home and take care of the goddamned kids for a while and see how you like it?" She didn't mean the part about goddamned kids. You've never seen three cleaner, calmer, happier babies. Gloria sets the mark and they toe it, but she loves them to death.

After the third C-section, she had her tubes tied. She figured she might as well have it done since she was already opened up and would not try again for the son I was going to name after my father.

I quit pulling wire that spring, borrowed against the equity in the mobile home and put the money into stock for the shop I set up in the garage. I figured I'd start small and work my way into sporting goods. It was a fine location, just across the road from the state access to the pond. In spring and summer, I could sell worms and salmon eggs and fish tackle. In the fall, I could sell ammunition and hunting equipment. In the winter, shiners and snowmobile parts. And I'd have plenty of time for my own trapping, hunting, fishing. A salesman had to try out his own wares after all. No more of this two-weeks-forced-vacation-in-July shit. No more having to call in sick during deer season.

"Gloria," I said, "it takes time. We'll lose money before we make money. But honey . . . this *will* work out for us. This will be the best ever."

She said: "You are the biggest fool I have ever known."

She worried me about insurance, debt, losing the mobile home, losing the land my father and mother left me. What if the refrigerator breaks down? What if one of the kids gets sick? What if something happens to you?

"Nothing's going to happen to me." I pulled her onto my lap. I snugged her head between my shoulder and neck in the warm place where it fits. That's the thing about Gloria: no matter how she sputters or how many orders she gives or how mean she cuts me, she still fits. I rubbed her forehead to make the troubles go away, starting with a small circle in the middle and working my way out to her temples, the way I do when she has a sick headache. "This will be the best ever," I said. "Promise."

Gloria baked bread, pies, and cookies to sell at the restaurant. I told her we ought to try a display right in the bait shop, but the first time I mentioned it she got mad. And the next time she cried. In November, when business slowed, I closed down for a couple of weeks. This gave me time to get the wood in and do some hunting. Gloria was worked up about the wood. Too green, she said, and too far from the house, and not enough of it. I built a cord-wood mountain by the back door. "Some of it's green now," I said, "but it'll dry fast in the sun."

"That's how the Indians dried their wood," I told the babies, "and don't you be climbing on it or it'll tumble down on your head and you might get hurt."

After Thanksgiving, I shot a big doe on the back side of Dunfey Hill. You'd think that would have pleased my wife—but no. She took the attitude that the deer just made more work for her and the girls didn't even like venison.

"Stew it," I said. "They'll never know the difference."

"Stew it yourself," she said.

In my spare time I set out a trap line. In three weeks I caught four foxes, one blanket beaver and a near-blanket, two mink, and fourteen muskrats. By Christmas the mortgage was paid up-to-date, so I could give Gloria fifty dollars to blow on the babies.

"The next mink I catch," I told her, "I'm not going to sell. I'm going to have it tanned and made into a collar for you." A mink collar is a beautiful thing. My father had one made for my mother once. The tanner inserted glass eyes and, for a fastener, sewed a clip where the jaw would have been. My mother wore it over her blue wool coat, with the jaw clipped to the tail as though the mink were biting itself in the ass. Seeing my mother with that collar around her neck made me feel rich and proud.

Gloria didn't want a mink collar. She said, "Forget it." She said, "I am not your mother. I am nothing like your mother." Today, she packed up the kids and went to live with her folks. "I've had it," she said. Her bitterness spoiled her beauty. I've been noticing that for a long time.

She said she's got a job full time in the office at the wire plant. She learned typing and shorthand in school and evidently is still pretty good at it. She's going to leave the babies at the day care.

I made some calls and learned it was Joe Blow, now assistant plant manager, who'd put in the good word for her. His evil eye has been on my wife for a long time. It's just one more way for him to get at me. I consider revenge. But after six and a half hours of sitting miserable in the dark and cold of the shop, I figure freezing myself sick is not the way to get it. I see there's no sense in this. Freezing myself will not hurt Joe Blow. Freezing myself will not bring Gloria and the babies back. It will not change who I am and the life I live. Morning soon. The ice fishermen will be pounding at the door.

But I cannot face the empty mobile home yet, so I stay put, stoking a small fire with the flue in upright and the stove doors wide open. I watch the flames. The fire is not hot enough for comfort, just to keep my teeth from chattering so I can hear myself think, just so I can watch the flames lick and lash one another.

I sit here remembering another cold night—a night as cold as this one and almost as lonely. It was the year my father bought a new Polaris Charger snowmobile—a machine I still own. There it sits behind the shop, hasn't been registered since I-don't-know-when, hasn't run since I-don't-know-when. But there it sits and there it will continue to sit as long as I have any say-so.

It was the only new vehicle my father ever owned. Always there were secondhand pick-up trucks, motorcycles, second-hand boats. In other years there would be secondhand snow-mobiles too, a free-air with a blown engine, an electric-start Arctic Cat with carburetor problems and no gumption, a Snow-jet he tried to get my mother to ride and which he named his little poppin' bug because it was so quiet and reliable. But the first snowmobile he ever owned was a new one, because there were no secondhand ones to be had.

Where he got the money, I don't know, but I felt rich and proud riding behind my father on that beautiful machine. We followed logging roads and others "Closed Subject to Gates and Bars." We bushwhacked trails straight through the woods to wherever we wanted to go. We skimmed the ponds. After a while, when the machine wasn't quite so new, he let me drive.

It was the year New Hampshire decided to trade fisher cats for wild turkeys with some state down south—North Carolina maybe, or South Carolina, something like that. Fish and Game would transport the fisher cats south and the turkeys north, hoping for a good strong transplant. The state would pay for a live fisher cat what a trapper would get for the fur, without the trouble of skinning and stretching. And I think my father liked the idea of getting money for an animal without having to kill it. Like me, he admired the animals he trapped. But it was hard to catch fisher cats live, hard to lure them into the box traps, hard to cover your own scent so they wouldn't be spooked. Only the best trappers could pull it off.

It was a cold night, well below zero—I want to say forty below but it might have been only thirty-five or it might have been fifty. My father had no chance that day to check the live trap located three and a quarter miles straight out behind the camp; he'd been busy all afternoon with the beaver sets in the backwater. Doesn't take long to check a beaver set when there's nothing in it. But when you do catch one, you have to haul the carcass out of the water on the long wire, then reset the trap under the ice with the pulp sticks arranged so the beaver will swim just so and get caught high up. A foot-caught beaver, if she doesn't drown right away, will twist the foot off and swim away. Then you've got trouble: a three-footed beaver setting off your traps on a regular basis, but almost impossible to catch.

My father would not allow the live trap to go unchecked even one day. He said if an animal happened to get caught, it would be cruel to leave her too long. My mother said, "You go with your father tonight, Richard." She was afraid of the cold, I think. She was afraid to have either of us out alone in forty-below weather. Especially after dark.

My father said, "Come on, Richie. But dress up warm."

My mother found the old coat in the closet. It had belonged to my uncle who flew the hump during World War II, a military-issue coat. The outside was smooth khaki, the lining pure wool. It was a big, heavy coat, which wrapped around me twice and hung to the floor. "Turn the collar up around your face," my mother said, "and tie the button." The collar was sheepskin. "Pull your hat down over your ears."

"I can't even walk in this coat," I said. "I feel foolish."

My father pulled his own hat down and tucked a scarf around his face. All I could see was the hard white bridge of his nose and the shine of his eyes. "Come on, Richie," he said. "If we don't hit the trail now, we won't be back until tomorrow."

By the time we reached the live trap, my feet ached with cold, though the rest of me felt all right. My boots, exposed to the wind on the running boards of the Polaris, just weren't insulated enough for forty-below, not even with felts and wool socks. My fingers were numb inside my gloves inside my mittens inside the pockets of my coat—but they didn't hurt yet. My face was stiff but not frozen because my father's bulk broke the wind as I hunched behind him on the machine.

The Polaris liked the cold. It sucked in the freezing air and wound up to speed with ease. My father drove fast, me bouncing around behind, the sledge and the pack basket secured with ropes and bouncing even further behind. I supposed he'd notice if I bounced off, but I wasn't positive.

It was hard to breathe as we raced through the night. Every breath caught in my nose and throat, the cold a continuing shock to my insides.

But luck was with us. The wire box was full. It was full of one bright-eyed, black-furred bundle of pure fear. Silent. As small as she could make herself. My father and I stood silent too, awed somehow—the living animal so much more impressive than the dead ones we were used to, the ones that hung limp from coni-bears on the down side of leaning birches.

We shone the flashlight in her eyes and tried to quiet our hard breathing for the silence of deep woods on a frozen night. I took a step forward. My boot crunched the frozen snow loud as gunshots, but the fisher cat did not move. She made no sound. The light bounced off her eyes.

We wrapped the whole box in a blanket and lifted it onto the sledge. She was dead weight inside, clinging to the wire with her toenails, fighting the tilt. My father worked the straps with his bare hands. I wondered how he could stand the cold, why his muscles still responded, why his red skin didn't just crack open. But he snugged each strap so the box wouldn't tip or slide on the long ride home, so our prize would be as safe and comfortable as possible.

"Well," he said, when all was secure and we were ready to head out. "I guess we've gone and done something this time, haven't we, Richie?"

"She's a beauty," I said.

"She's scared to death," he said. "And she'd bite your finger off if you stuck it in there—she'd bite clear to the bone. That's how scared she is."

We mounted the machine. The engine sounds filled my head, which snapped forward so my face touched the wool of my father's back. Where we were going the headlight shone bright enough: a tunnel through the trees. Up and down the light moved as the track hit a ridge, as we plunged into a gully and out the other side.

I craned my neck and shoulders to check behind, to make sure the box was in place. I touched the rope with my leather mitten and felt the tremor, the pull of the loaded sledge. I felt the cold deep, as deep as the night my wife and babies left me.

The taillight made a red glow that reached just to the box, but no further. I could barely make out the soft corners where the blanket folded over. I could barely make out the curve of the sledge.

Beyond. Beyond was black like I've never seen since. Beyond the small glow of the taillight I could sense nothing but a universe of darkness.

I knew my father lived and breathed just inches away. I knew I was not alone. I knew the headlight guided us along the rough trail we had bushwhacked with our own hands. I heard the roar of our beautiful new machine making its way toward home. But I experienced, for a moment, only the darkness behind. And I realized that if the machine faltered, if the engine missed a beat, if we hesitated, when we hesitated, the dark would engulf us.

⚑ Ada Among the Dogs

Today the dogs sound closer than ever—too close, as though some have broken free and formed a pack. But instead of retreating home, Ada walks toward them, toward the soggy ravine beyond the next wooded hill where they sound like they might be. Their voices are frenzied. Have they run down a doe? Are they tearing one of the neighbor's lambs to pieces?

Every day she walks. When she walks she often hears dogs talking to each other. Their voices carry: deep-throated howls, wails and yaps, threats and warnings. Dogs she has never seen, chained in the hidden yards of neighbors she hardly knows. In cold weather she goes out early to gather kindling. The stove is too small to hold the fire overnight, so in the morning, after Matt leaves, it is her job to build it up again, hot enough to burn creosote from the pipe, but not to drive the chill from this drafty house-trailer, with its cardboard walls and tin siding. If it gets too cold, the baseboard heaters kick in, but if the electric bill is high at the end of the month, that's her fault. So she goes out early to break brittles off standing pine and snap branches over her knee. Often she hears dogs in the distance, one talking to another, talking to another—complaints, confessions, supplications passed through the woods dog to dog, she imagines, all the way to Canada.

She and Matt have no close neighbors on the road. The dirt turns to mud in the spring making it nearly impassable without four-wheel drive. This pleases him. The Bronco gets him out all right, but in mud season nobody comes to call, he's sure of it. Other times, Ada sweeps the tracks away as best she can—even if they're only the tracks of the meter-reader or Jehovah's Witnesses. Tracks in the yard lead to interrogation. He'll want to know who, how long they stayed, what they said, how they said it. "I'm thinking about you all the time, Ada," he says. "Every minute of the miserable day."

There was a time when she told him everything, in self-defense. If she told him everything, she figured, there would be nothing for him to discover and twist. Yes, Frank LeBel stopped in to pick up Matt's house jacks, on his way to Macon. He needed them to fix the rotted sills at his girl friend's. It was hot, he wanted a beer. He asked for one. No, she hadn't drunk a beer with him. He stood in the yard and drank from the can. He said weren't the white lilacs pretty and wanted to pick a few to bring to Cheryl since she was mad at him over nothing. She just got mad sometimes for no reason, but a batch of flowers might turn her around. That and the sill work. No, he didn't come in the house. She brought the beer out to him, and some wet paper towels to wrap the lilacs.

"Frank knew damn well I was cutting cordwood up to Lacey's today," Matt said to his fists, red-knuckled on the enamel tabletop. "He knew I wouldn't be anywhere around, that son-of-a-bitch." Then he looked wild-eyed at her across the table. She did not react. Her expression was as flat as her two hands on the tabletop, fingers spread and still. He tapped the back of her hand with two fingers. "If I hadn't noticed the can of beer gone," he said, "you wouldn't even mentioned it, would you?" Now he was squeezing her hand. His ragged fingernails dug deep, but her face did not change.

"He was on his way to Macon and he needed the jacks," she said.

The screen door snapped shut behind him. Out to the wood

pile. Wood needs splitting. Split white pine, red oak, yellow birch. Smoke a cigarette. Split some more. A seeding of cigarette butts, white among the wood chips. Even inside the trailer, with the doors and windows closed against evening damp, wrapped in a blanket, rocking in the maplewood chair, she could feel his rage.

Another road, the Old Turnpike, swings around behind their land almost a mile straight out through the woods, between them and the river. It is there, near the Old Turnpike, that a sheep fence winds through the trees and beyond it the trees gradually thin to meadow. Sometimes mornings when she walks along the fence, she hears the sheep crackling the bushes. She walks toward the sounds but, sensing her, the sheep scatter. She sees their cauliflower backs disappearing in the underbrush.

Today, the frenzied voices of the dogs seem to be coming from a place she knows where the fence dips into wetland; where the trees are stunted from too much water, dead and dying; where the alders grow thick. She pictures that place and walks toward it, though there are no paths to follow, though she knows dogs can be dangerous. Still, she is drawn to whatever trouble has sharpened the voices.

She walks terrain rough with heeled-over trees, brush, ledge, and bogs skimmed with ice too thin to hold her weight. This land is swollen with hills. Usually she wanders ravine to ravine, choosing the course of least resistance, but today, drawn to the dogs, almost hurrying, she seeks the direct route over the top of a steep hill, one hand under her belly, the other seeking balance and momentum in hemlock boughs and the thin, strong trunks of young beech.

Drumlins, her father named the hummocks on similar terrain in the place where she grew up, fifty miles north as the crow flies, fifty miles due north through these woods. Her father, who loved to tease, said side-hill wampuses patrolled the drumlins. The wampuses looked like Bigfoot except they had one leg shorter than the other to keep their balance walking always in the same direction on the steep side-hills. "Watch out for them wampuses," he said. "Get on the flat or the ice if a wampus is after you. The short leg slows 'em down on level going."

Foolish talk from a man she remembers when she walks in the woods because that's where he spent his time, that's where she spent time with him. She's heard nothing from him or of him since she left home with Matt, whom her father did not respect, whom her father punched in the collarbone after the curses ran out. Matt pushed her father down then, in his own front yard where neighbors might have seen, pushed with two hands, almost gently, and toppled him into the azalea. The branches broke his fall and petals fell on his bald head, on his forehead striped with sunburn, on his nose, on his shirt. He looked like he wanted to laugh, there in the azalea, his knees by his ears. She wanted to laugh, too, and—thinking back— she imagines that if she had laughed, if she and her father had been able to laugh together, maybe everything would have been different. Maybe. But over her father's head, above the azalea, she saw her mother's face at the window, as close as a face could get to the glass without touching it. Her mother's face filled the window, jaw stubborn set, eyes dark with judgment, the bloody mote in her right eye gleaming. Her mother, silent and, at last, satisfied that her daughter was as selfish and sinful as she'd always imagined her to be.

Ada held tight as Matt barreled the Chevy truck too fast down the pot-hole road that would take them from the house to the village to the interstate. She didn't look at his face. She didn't look back either, at her father climbing out of the azalea, at the window that framed the oval of her mother's face. She studied her fingers spread over the dash, her thumbs digging the yellow insulation which puffed through the split in the vinyl.

Seventeen days later, she would miscarry, but by then it was already too late. She supposes the news must have got back to her parents, through Matt's people, but she heard nothing from them. Now the silence has gone on so long rot has set in and moss grown over. Silence separates and unites them, and it seems like that's the way it will always be.

Once when she was younger, twelve or thirteen years old, out alone checking her father's trap line in the frozen swamp, the snowmobile broke down in the shadow of a drumlin like the one she skirts now, too steep to climb, as she presses on toward the dogs. The snowmobile broke down at dusk when the air was white and raw with snow on the way. The dead trees, silvered with weathering, stood like sentinels on the ice and her father's stories filled her imagination. Though she knew it was just his foolish talk, she felt as though she were being watched. There on the edge of the swamp as the shadows took hold, she faced the dilemma of walking the four miles home in the dark or waiting in the cold until someone noticed she was a long time gone, guessed she needed help, and came for her. She saw a shadow slide from one sentinel tree to another. She heard movement among the hemlocks that crowned the drumlin. Strange to feel afraid in the woods, where she usually felt safe, confident that if *they* came after her—the pale *they* of her nightmares—she could hide in a crevice between boulders, the pocket under low fir branches, a hollow in the earth. But that evening, she didn't try to hide. She knew she couldn't hide. She ran from the moving shadows and rustling hemlocks. She ran and ran into the spongy darkness toward home.

She does not feel afraid now. She is not afraid of the displaced dogs who change the familiar woods with their too-close voices, though she knows she ought to be. She crests the last ridge and there they are, all at once, just beyond the sheep fence in the ravine, separated from her by a grid of heavy-gauge wire. Bigger than she'd imagined, they dominate the landscape of fence, underbrush, and swamp maple. Three big dogs—one black, one gold, one white. The white one has thrust a leg and its massive head through the fence and seems trapped in the grid. The other two leap against the fence, leap against the trapped dog, leap against each other. They want to be where Ada is. Straggly hair drips dirty water. Now they spot her. Now they are barking up at her.

She freezes on the ridge, staring down. The black dog, upright on sinewy hind legs, claws the wire, claws the shoulder of the white dog which yipes in pain. The gold dog circles, nips the white dog from behind, leaps away, nips again. The white dog growls and snaps but can't get its big square head around far enough to drive the aggressor off.

Ada knows she should turn, walk back the way she came, leave them. She knows the dogs could hurt her, knock her down, maul her, but she doesn't believe it. She sleepwalks down the hill toward them, vaguely aware of the pain in the muscles of her lower abdomen, taut with the weight that will be Matt's child—the final link between them—if she carries it through the winter. She knows she is pregnant, but she doesn't believe it. She has tried to make the child real in her mind, to imagine its soft bones and flesh. Sometimes she lies on the bed and listens to the lullaby bells of the red-and-yellow mobile Matt bought at the neighbor's yard sale, white-faced clowns circling and bobbing. She tries to imagine an infant, a girl or a boy, the shape of it, the weight of it in her arms. She tries to imagine holding it close, the warmth of its breath. But there is nothing, nothing. She wonders if her mother suffered the same

failure of imagination. She wonders if her mother ever believed in her at all. *Daddy did*, she thinks. *He misses me. He
would come for me if he knew.*

Ada stumbles toward the dogs and the neighbor's land and
the fence she has never crossed. In her mind, a plan has formed
to free the white dog—to guide its leg back through the mesh,
to stretch the wire away from its head. What has stirred these
dogs up so? Why do they press the fence with such despera-
tion? What are they chasing? What are they running from?

When she slip-slides finally into the ravine, she sees how the
dogs' wet hair slicks their legs, accentuating bone and muscle.
They pant, muzzles dripping a froth of saliva. Blood stains the
white dog's chin and chest. She thinks it must be blood, though
it is not as deeply red as she would expect, more pink than red.
Blood too on the gold dog's paws, blood on its mouth, in its
mouth, and the teeth bared to warn her away.

She takes two steps toward them and even as she moves forward, she's wondering why? She's thinking: *Turn around, Ada.
Turn back before it's too late.* But the white dog whines for help.
A young dog, it appears to be, young enough perhaps to expect
kindness. "What's wrong?" she says. "You stuck? What's wrong,
honey? Where do you belong?"

The two free dogs back away from Ada as she approaches
the fence, one cautious step at a time. The gold dog growls.
The black dog studies her silently, its mouth partly open, black
lips curling away from long teeth. She claps her hands: "Go
home!" When she claps again and runs toward the fence, the
dogs turn and flee, abandoning their companion—running out of the alders and swamp maple, up into the open, into
the meadow rising. They pause under a solitary elm, leafless,
umbrella-branched. They pause and turn to look at her. She
waves her arms wildly: "Go. Go now!" Now she is within an
arm's length of the white dog, who cannot flee. Now she sees

that some of the blood may be its own, hair torn from its shoulder, a long, ragged gash—the mark of barbed wire?

She holds out her open hand, palm up. The dog stiffens. Its eyes—the color of fog —focus not on her hand but her face. She raises her hand, then slowly lowers it to curve over the dog's broad skull. Her fingers span its width. The hair is stiff and damp. The dog trembles.

"You've got a collar," she says. "You belong to somebody. Somebody loves you, huh?" She slides her hand down the side of the dog's soft face and into the thick hair of its neck. "I'm just going to reach around here. . . . It's all right. . . ."

Then she hears the shot, they both hear it—not the pop of a BB gun, but the deadly song, not far away, of a high-powered rifle—first the blast, then the sustained echo. Even before the echo dies, the rifle sings again.

One thing Matt shares with her father is the philosophy that a dog running deer deserves to be shot. "The pack'll hamstring 'em first, then when the deer is down they rip it to pieces," Matt told her. Her father, who kept the family's freezer stocked with venison, thought nothing deserved to die that way, helpless on the ground, the dogs circling. To him, that was unnatural cruelty. Either man would kill any dog he caught running deer, except perhaps his own.

Startled by the shots, frightened by Ada's reaction to the shots, the white dog lunges, pushes against her with its extended leg, toenails raking, and when she throws out her arm to catch her balance, the dog tears her sweater and finds her flesh in one snap of its jaw. Even as teeth scrape bone, she thinks, *an accident, that's all—the dog is scared, that's all—he doesn't mean to hurt me.* It is over in an instant, the clamp of jaw, the shot of pain, then the release. She notices the holes where the skin has broken. She turns her wrist, fascinated by the punctures, a matched set on the other side. Do the wounds go all the way through? She sees her blood, seeping. She feels the baby move. "Oh my God," she says. She spreads her fingers over her stomach, feels the pressure and release, hard and soft, her baby rolling.

Somehow in its lunge and recoil the dog has pulled itself free. The fence still separates them, and Ada feels safe, safe enough. The dog snuffles at the ground, then lifts its big head and muddy nose to sniff the air for its companions. Catching the scent, it hesitates only a moment, then runs where the others ran, through the brush, to the open space where meadow begins, past the umbrella elm, and out of sight.

Ada is sitting on the cold ground, her knees folded under her. She holds her throbbing wrist to her chest and presses with her good hand the heart side of the wound. The white dog's dark leather collar hangs from the fence by its broken buckle. *All right*, she thinks. *We'll be all right.* Dry yellow leaves that should have fallen long ago rattle over her head in a chilling gust of ground wind. It is then that Ada begins to howl.

ACKNOWLEDGMENTS

The author acknowledges the following publications in which some of her stories first appeared:

Potato Eyes: "Minna Runs for Selectman," "The White Room"

Echoes: "Jim's Boat," "The Fisher Cat."

Northern Review: "Three"

Bone and Flesh: "Etta Walks"

The Cream City Review: "Ada Among the Dogs"

Yankee: "The Widow and the Trapper," "Fishing with George," "Walking the Trapline," and "Saturday Night at the Hi-View Drive-In." Reprinted with permission from *Yankee* Magazine, published in Dublin, N.H.

"The Widow and the Trapper," "Peach Baby Food Sandwiches," "Walking the Trapline," 'Saturday Night at the Hi-View Drive-In," and "The White Room" were collected in *Wood Heat: Stories from Up North*, by Rebecca Rule (Troy, Maine: Nightshade Press, 1992).

Rebecca Rule was born in Concord, New Hampshire, and brought up in Boscawen, moved down the road to Northwood when she grew up, and there she stays. Others in her family have hunted, trapped, lumbered, railroaded, milled, carpentered. She writes about those things. Others in her family catch a lot of fish. She catches a few, and writes about it. She loves and hates small-town politics. Her experiences on the policy advisory committee, recreation commission, school board, PTA, Friends of the Libraries, and Historical Society and her observations (and confrontations) at selectmen's meetings, budget committee hearings, and town and school district meetings inspire her fiction. She writes to preserve what she knows of rural New Hampshire and to understand her community and herself. She writes because living the life of a writer is clearly the best revenge.

LIBRARY OF CONGRESS CATALOGING-IN-PUBLICATION DATA
Rule, Rebecca.

The best revenge : short stories / Rebecca Rule.

p.   cm.—(Hardscrabble books)

ISBN 0–87451–702–8 (cl); ISBN 1–58465–373–6 (pa)

1. New England—Social life and customs—Fiction. I. Title.
II. Series.

PS3568.U422B47   1995

813'.54—dc20   94–40944